A
FORBIDDEN
PASSION

A FORBIDDEN PASSION

Stories

CRISTINA PERI ROSSI

Translated by

MARY JANE TREACY

CLEIS
PRESS

Originally published in Spanish as *Una pasión prohibida*, Editorial Seix
Barral, s.a., Barcelona, 1986, 1987, © 1986 by Cristina Peri Rossi

Translation © 1993 by Mary Jane Treacy. First Edition. Published in the
United States by Cleis Press Inc., P.O. Box 8933, Pittsburgh, Pennsylvania
15221, and P.O. Box 14684, San Francisco, California 94114

Cover and interior design: Pete Ivey
Cleis logo art: Juana Alicia

ISBN: 0-939416-67-0 (cloth); 0-939416-68-9 (paper)
Printed in the United States of America
10 9 8 7 6 5 4 3 2 1

Library of Congress Cataloging-in-Publication Data

Peri Rossi, Cristina, 1941–
    [Pasión prohibida. English]
    A forbidden passion / Cristina Peri Rossi : translated by Mary Jane
Treacy. — 1st ed.
        p. cm.
    ISBN 0-939416-67-0 : $24.95. — ISBN 0-939416-68-9 (pbk.) : $9.95
    I. Title.
PQ8520.26.E74P313   1993
863—dc20   92-44010
                                                                CIP

Man is a useless passion.

—*Jean-Paul Sartre*

Contents

Introduction

THE FRENCH PHILOSOPHER Jean-Paul Sartre defined human existence as a useless passion always headed toward failure. This definition belonged to an especially somber period of history after the Second World War, when Europe, formerly the cradle of civilization, found itself divided and destroyed by conflicts, rivalries and perverse nationalisms. But the origins of this definition were even more remote: the pessimist philosophers of Ancient Greece had warned about the deceptive nature of human passions, created by the gods to bring mortals to their perdition. The definition says nothing about the pleasure of the illusory, however, of the happiness of feeling the force of desire, without which there is no life. Inebriated, enraptured by throbbing dreams and the search for the objects of our passion, we human beings are arrows shot out into time and space to catch the impossible. The building of houses and bridges, scaling of mountains, journeys, explorations, investigations, collection of objects and attempts at seduction: almost all human activity is an anxious tension reaching toward this object that always escapes us, the object of desire.

From 1984 to 1985 I wrote a group of stories at once full of irony and tenderness, in which Atlas tired of holding the world on his shoulders, a girl sang in the desert, a city fought for two hundred years over which side of a river would be selected to begin construction of a bridge, a man tried to thank another for a favor, a woman wanted to dream and a traveler was lost in an unknown city. I realized that many of the stories had a common foundation: the fever of passion and the great and small failures in the attainment of its object. These short stories were peopled by men and women battling destiny (the most ancient and always renewed combat), supported by their zeal to fulfill their desire: inflamed patriots or lovers, inveterate travelers, women poets and heroes forgotten by history. These were cosmopolitan, universal stories; the excitement of fulfilling dreams renders the circumstances of time and place irrelevant.

I collected them in a book entitled *A Forbidden Passion*, published for the first time the following year. They enjoyed an excellent reception by the public and by critics; the volume has been in print continuously since that time.

I think that literature is an act of mercy towards a human race that is ignorant, proud, unhappy and subject to excessive limitations. The most satiric episodes in this book (fratricidal fights obscured by political rhetoric, false morality, egotism disguised as generosity, etc.) do not lessen my feelings of tenderness towards the characters and their situations. In the end, this should be the only attitude that God has for his creatures. I have been the little goddess of this book.

CRISTINA PERI ROSSI
Barcelona, July 1992

The Fallen Angel

THE ANGEL PLUMMETED TO EARTH exactly like the Russian satellite that while spying on the movements of the American Tenth Fleet lost height when it should have been thrust into a strong nine hundred and fifty kilometer orbit. It fell exactly like the American satellite that while spying on the movements of the Russian fleet in the North Sea also fell to earth after a wrong move. But while both of these incidents brought about innumerable catastrophes—part of Canada turned into desert, several types of fish became extinct, local people's teeth crumbled, and neighboring lands became polluted—the angel's fall didn't cause any ecological disturbance. Because it was weightless (a theological mystery that cannot be doubted upon pain of heresy), it didn't destroy anything in its wake, not the trees on the road nor the electric wires; it didn't cause interference in TV programs nor in radio stations; it didn't open up a crater in the face of the earth, nor did it poison the waters. No, it just settled down on the sidewalk and stayed there without moving, confused and with a terrible case of motion sickness.

At first no one noticed it. That was because the inhabitants of the place, sick and tired of nuclear catastrophes, had lost the ability to be surprised and were busy putting the city back together, cleaning out debris, analyzing food and water, putting houses back up and finding furniture, just like ants when the ant hill is destroyed, but with much more sadness.

"I think it's an angel," said the first observer, contemplating the little figure fallen at the base of a statue beheaded in the last conflagration. Actually, it was a rather small angel with muti-lated wings (it's not known if this was due to the fall) and an unhappy expression.

A woman walked right by, so busy pushing a baby carriage that she didn't notice it. But a hungry stray walked right up and then stopped short: that thing, whatever it was, didn't smell, and anything that doesn't smell can't really exist, so the dog wasn't going to waste its time. Slowly (it was lame) it did an about face.

Another man stopped, curious, and looked the angel over cautiously but didn't reach out to touch it, afraid that it might be radioactive.

"I think it's an angel," repeated the first observer, who by now felt as if he had first dibs on the visitor.

"It's pretty beaten up," noted the latest observer. "I don't think it has any use at all."

At the end of an hour a small group had assembled. No one touched it; instead they chatted among themselves and put forth a variety of opinions though nobody doubted that it *was* an angel. As a matter of fact, most thought that it was a fallen angel, although they couldn't come to any agreement on the reasons for its descent. Several hypotheses were bandied about.

"It may have sinned," said a young man made bald by the pollution.

It was possible. Now then, what kind of sin could an angel commit? It was too skinny for the sin of gluttony; it was too ugly for the sin of pride; according to one of those present, angels didn't have parents so it was impossible for it to have dishonored them; it clearly lacked sexual organs so lust, too, was rejected. Insofar as curiosity was concerned, it didn't give the smallest sign of having any.

"Let's ask it in writing," suggested an elderly man with a cane under his arm.

The proposal was accepted and a clerk was named, but when he was ready, with great formality, to begin his task, a discouraging question arose: what language do angels speak? Nobody knew the answer, although it seemed to them that as a matter of courtesy the visiting angel should be familiar with the language they spoke in that region of the country (which was, by the way, an uncommon dialect of which they were inexplicably proud).

Meanwhile the angel gave few signs of life, although nobody could say for sure what would be signs of life in an angel. It stayed in its original position, perhaps because it was comfortable or perhaps because it couldn't move, and the blue tone of its skin neither lightened nor darkened.

"What's its race?" asked a young man who had arrived late and who leaned over the others' shoulders to get a better view.

No one knew how to answer him. The angel was not pure Aryan, which caused some disappointment; it wasn't black, which made some hearts warmer; it wasn't Indian (can anyone imagine an Indian angel?) or yellow: it was really blue, and there weren't any prejudices yet about this color, even though some showed signs of forming with incredible speed.

The age of angels was another problem. Although one group asserted that angels were always children, the appearance of the angel neither confirmed nor refuted this theory.

But the most surprising thing was the color of the angel's eyes. No one noticed until someone said, "The prettiest part is its blue eyes."

Then a woman who was near the angel said, "What are you saying? Can't you see that they are pink?"

A science professor, happening by, leaned down to observe the eyes better and exclaimed: "You are all wrong. They are green."

Everyone saw a different color. For that reason, they deduced that the eyes weren't one special color, but rather made up of all colors.

"This will bring it problems when it has to give proof of identification," thought a retired bureaucrat who had false teeth and a big gold ring on his right hand.

There was no doubt about its sex; the angel was sexless, neither female nor male, unless (a hypothesis that was readily rejected) its genitals were hidden in some other place. This bothered some of those present quite a bit. After a period of real confusion about the sexes and unfettered promiscuity, the pendulous movement of history (simple as a compass) had returned us to the happy era of differentiated, perfectly recognizable sexes. But the angel seemed uninformed of this evolution.

"Poor thing," commented a pleasant lady who had been leaving her house to go shopping when she ran into the angel. "I'd bring it to my home to recuperate, but I have two adolescent daughters, and if no one can tell me if it's a man or a woman, I won't do it. It just wouldn't be right for it to live with my daughters."

"I have a dog and a cat," murmured a well-dressed gentleman with an agreeable baritone voice. "They'd get very jealous if I took it home with me."

"Moreover one would have to know something about its background," proclaimed a man with rabbit teeth, a narrow forehead and tortoise-shell glasses, dressed all in brown. "Maybe a permit is needed." He had the appearance of a police informant, and this displeased those present so they didn't answer him.

"And nobody knows what it eats," whispered a nice man with a very clean appearance who smiled, showing a line of bright white teeth.

"They eat herring," asserted a beggar who was always drunk and whom everybody normally scorned on account of his body odor. No one paid any attention to him now.

"I'd like to know what it thinks," said a man who had the bright look of those with a curious spirit.

But the majority of those present were of the opinion that angels didn't think.

Someone noted that the angel seemed to move its leg slightly, which caused great expectations.

"Surely it wants to walk," commented an old woman.

"I never heard of angels walking," said a woman dressed in fuchsia, with wide shoulders and hips and a narrow, somewhat skeptical mouth. "It should fly."

"This one is broken," responded the man who had been the first to approach.

The angel again moved almost imperceptibly.

"Maybe it needs help," murmured a young student with a melancholy air.

"I advise you not to touch it. It's gone through space and can be full of radiation," observed a quick-witted man who was proud of his common sense.

Suddenly an alarm sounded. It was time for the air raid drill, and everyone was supposed to run to shelters in the basements of buildings. The procedure was intended to take place as quickly as possible. Not an instant was to be lost. The group dissolved rapidly, leaving the angel behind.

The city emptied in a few seconds, but the alarm kept sounding. Cars were left on sidewalks, stores closed, plazas emptied, movie houses darkened, and televisions became mute. The angel made another small movement.

A middle-aged woman, with slouched shoulders and an old red coat that at one time had been the height of fashion, walked calmly down the street as if deliberately ignoring the sound of the sirens. Her pulse was somewhat erratic, she had blue circles around her eyes and her skin was very white, still rather youthful. She had gone out initially for cigarettes, but once in the street, she decided not to pay any attention to the air raid. The idea of taking a walk through the abandoned, empty city was very seductive.

When she got to the beheaded statue, she saw a bundle on the ground next to the pedestal.

"Gosh! An angel," she cried.

An airplane flew over her head and dumped out a sort of chalk dust. Instinctively, she looked up and then turned her gaze below to the silent bundle that could barely move.

"Don't get frightened," the woman told the angel. "They're disinfecting the city." The dust covered the shoulders of her red coat, her brown, rather disheveled hair, the dull leather of her worn shoes.

"If it's all the same to you, I'll keep you company for a little while," said the woman and sat down by its side. In truth, she was a rather intelligent woman with a great sense of independence who tried not to bother anyone. Still she knew how to value a good friendship as well as a nice solitary walk, good tobacco, a good book and a good opportunity.

"This is the first time I've met an angel," commented the woman, lighting a cigarette. "I suppose it doesn't happen very often."

As she expected, the angel didn't say a thing.

"I suppose, too," she continued, "that you didn't have any intention of paying us this visit. You simply fell due to some mechanical defect. What doesn't happen in millions of years happens in one day, my mother used to say. And it happened precisely to you. Surely you realize that any angel who fell out of the sky would feel just as you do. Certainly you weren't able to pick your landing spot."

The alarm had stopped and an imposing silence filled the city. She hated this silence and tried not to hear it. She took another drag on her cigarette.

"You live as you can. I'm not happy in this place either, but I could say the same about many others I know. It's not a question of choice, but of endurance. And I don't have too much patience, believe me. I'd like to know if someone is going to miss you. Surely someone will have noticed your fall. An unforeseen accident in the smooth running of the universe, a change in fixed plans, just like a bomb bursting into flames or a faucet dripping. One chance in billions, but nevertheless, it does happen, isn't that so?"

She didn't expect an answer and she wasn't concerned about the angel's silence. Sometimes she thought that it was wrong to construct the universe on the invention of language. However, she felt the silence that was now overwhelming the city was like an invasion by an enemy army that takes over a territory like a multifaceted star slowly falling apart.

"You'll see right away," she informed the angel, "that here we go by the rules of time and space, which nevertheless don't reduce our insecurity. I think this will be an even more difficult blow to you than your fall to earth. If you can distinguish bodies, you'll see that we divide ourselves into men and women, a distinction that has no importance because we all die without exception and death is the most significant event in our lives."

She put out her cigarette. It had been unwise to keep it lit during the air raid but her philosophy included some snubbing of the rules as a way of rebelling. The angel suggested another little movement, but seemed to cut it off before finishing. She looked at it with pity.

"Poor little thing!" she exclaimed. "I understand you don't feel very much like moving. But the drill lasts almost an hour. It will be better if you have learned to move by then; if not, you could be run over by a car, asphyxiated by a gas leak, arrested for causing a public disturbance and interrogated by the secret police. And I advise you not to go up on that pedestal—" (it seemed to her that the angel was looking at the top of the column as if it might be a comfortable resting spot) "because politics in our city are very volatile, and today's hero is tomorrow's traitor. Moreover, this city doesn't raise monuments to foreigners."

All of a sudden out of a side street, a group of soldiers, dense as beetles, began to move, taking over the sidewalks and highways and crawling through the trees. They moved in an order that surely had been prearranged and they wore helmets that emitted strong beams of light.

"They're here," sighed the woman with resignation. "It's certain they are going to arrest me again. I don't know what kind of heaven you fell from," she told the angel, "but these guys really seem to have climbed out of the hellish depths of the earth."

Just so, the beetles advanced slowly and surely.

She got up because she didn't like to be taken by surprise or to be touched too much. She took out of her purse a driver's license, an identification card, a housing registration, some food coupons, and then took a few resigned steps forward.

The angel got up on its feet. It slowly shook off the chalk dust that covered its legs and arms and tried to flex its muscles. Afterwards it wondered if anyone would miss the woman who had fallen before being violently forced into the armored car.

A Forbidden Passion

THEY SENT HIM TO EUROPE because he was in love. His father—who had no idea about affairs of the heart—thought that cities, monuments, museums and bridges would distract him. But the cities always had a letter of the alphabet, a bell tower, a plaza, a sound of water that reminded him of her; he found a torso or profile similar to hers each time he went to a museum; he found and lost her on every bridge—the arch at Locarno, the buttress at Avignon; trains transported him only from a memory of glass where she was reflected—Rimini—to a memory of water—Amstel—where he was able to see her again. He traveled as if in a dream. The names of the cities echoed in his mind; on repeating them, on turning them over and over, slowly the name of the woman he loved appeared. Barcelona and Bruges disappeared into the fog, Siena was the gold color of her hair, and the mermaids of Oslo—made of stone or lead—bent over at the waist just as she did. Years later he would say that he traveled like a sleepwalker. To catch a glimpse of her behind a gallery window in melancholy Berlin— the guide stubbornly took them to all the exhibits—and the next day to discover her in a café in Vienna, had all the obscure logic of dreams, whose strange truths are unquestionable. Once in Milan, he was signed to a youth basketball team about to go on the road. His fifteen years and meter eighty in height gave him an edge. He accepted because he had come to see that the trip's purpose was useless, and he hoped to repay his father's sacrifice with money, since he could not erase her memory.

He played without enthusiasm, and when he made baskets, he had the sensation that the ball never returned to the ground. Surely the force that he used to toss it into the air also took it off to that dreamlike place where he was floating, wildly in love with a woman who was twice his age, and where, too, floated the cities that passed by like so many cardboard stage sets as he looked out from trains and river boats. Fountains, monuments, aqueducts, castles, languages, he repeated them all like words in an unreal litany while remaining deep inside himself, jealously guarded, one single landscape, one single feeling.

The father was happy that his son was traveling on tour with a team from Milan, but the short messages he received on postcards from France and Spain kept him wary. The boy played and scored mechanically, happy to perform some tasks—breathe, rebound, pass the ball—like an automaton. It was then he learned that you can live half asleep without anyone noticing the difference. Performing everyday acts perfectly and frequently allowed him to keep intact his inner space; Venice, Athens and Nantes were just windows full of reflecting mirrors revealing the profile of his beloved in different lights, like a melody repeated in different keys. He fulfilled each step of the journey without anxiety now that the travel itinerary, broken down perfectly into many parts, did not challenge his internal geography. The rue des Voges, with all its watchmakers' shops, became the street where they walked after leaving school and where she first spoke to him about Pierre Reverdy. (He wrote down the name, awkward, ignorant, grieving his youth, his height, and his passage from the countryside to the city with only innocence as his passport.) And the Mediterranean bay where for the first time he ate crabs in their own sauce (a fact that he deposited on a postcard to his father—precision in external details being a wonderful safeguard from intimacy) in an instant turned into the Atlantic beach where for the first time—and this initiation had great importance—he had bathed with her.

The last night he didn't know if the fireworks were in celebration of the team's championship, the new year, a local festivity or some political triumph. ("Where are we?" he asked the trainer, only to make note of the place where he was supposedly eating, breathing and dressing. "In Genoa," answered the trainer, and it seemed strange and wonderful to the boy that, after having traveled through so many places and having sent a dozen postcards, he was once again at the port where he first arrived, dreamy and aloof.) His ship was sailing the next day, but this fact didn't excite him unduly; if he had never really left, if he had never really stopped seeing the woman he loved, if he had chatted with her in the Musée de l'Homme, in the Rose Gallery, on the Ponte Vecchio, then crossing the ocean again was like not having crossed it at all; he was holing up forever in his own internal time and space which no external event could change. Nevertheless, and in deference to others (and especially in order not to arouse suspicion), he filled his suitcases with souvenirs from the trip; pennants, miniature Eiffel Towers, letter openers from Toledo and silk handkerchiefs for his mother.

He wasn't at all disappointed not to see her at the entrance to the port among the lines of cars or among his classmates, who were waving a sign that said 'Welcome' in red letters. If he hadn't left, there was no reason for her to be waiting for him. For the same reason, neither he nor she had exchanged letters during this period. To seek out a print of a Bacon painting (it was she who taught him how to look at it, just as she got him to read Böll and to distinguish one seashell from another) and send it to her with words like "the impossible task of shaving or of forgetting you in a sink, in the National Gallery or here among the ducks at the Luxembourg Gardens," would have seemed clumsy, an unnecessary barrier in their lives.

In order to put everybody's mind at ease, his first conversations were full of those small details that display the traveler's experiences and awaken the envy of those who have not yet traveled. He had some words in Greek to show his mother that his time in Athens had not been misspent. He spoke of Adrian's ancient palace in Rome, of the cathedral of Santiago and of the beauty of a particular mountain village in a Swiss canton whose name he found difficult to pronounce. He recommended the typical dishes of each place, praised the efficiency of the European administrations and their legitimate governments. For his male listeners, avid for naughty details, he recalled a stroll through the outskirts of Amsterdam and a certain gallery of naked women in Hamburg. His father was beginning to believe that his savings had been well used. He remembered a bullfight in Madrid and the grape harvest in the French countryside, when the air was so full of perfume that the butterflies and bees became intoxicated and threw themselves against his cheeks. And the bicycle trails in London with pale blond girls in trousers crossing the avenues.

He gave gifts to everyone, showing a delicate sensitivity in his selection. And at night he retired to his room, tired from the trip, the long conversations, and the inevitable questions. He had promised his father a few hours earlier that he would begin training if they offered him a spot on one of the most important teams in the country. He had to make use of his conditioning and the experience gathered in Europe.

He jumped out the window as usual, without worrying about breaking an ankle, so important for future basketball tournaments. He paid no attention to the stars or the street lights, because in those long nights of sleeplessness, travel and dejection, the constellations had become interchangeable, and the pain of absence was the same under Orion's belt as under Ursa Major. As for street corners, he had learned that their only differences were in shape; some were at a right angle and others were round. Anguish, however, always had the same form: a tunnel without bottom, without light, endless.

He set off for the tavern, the only one he found open. It could have been in the rue de l'Eperon, on the bridge of Saint Barnabas, or some greasy dive in the Trastevere. But the fat man on duty was the same. Fat, ugly, sad, obliging. A basketball fan, too. He was there, as always, just like the boy. He ordered a beer just to ask for something, and paid the fat man with a ten thousand lira note. The man looked at the note without surprise.

"I don't know the current rate," he said.

The boy took out ten Swiss francs, a dollar and one hundred pesetas from an old wallet that had been attacked by the rain of many cities.

"Old pieces of paper," commented the fat man. "They're only good to paper the walls."

"I'll give them to you," the boy responded, placing the bills on the table. "When did you see her last?"

The fat man picked up the bills without interest. Money was all the same: dirty paper with drawings of kings and princes nobody remembered and who had become as wrinkled as their reputations.

"I'm not sure," the fat man told him. "Yesterday or perhaps a week ago. Genoa? Were you in Genoa? I think I may have relatives somewhere around there."

"Parma, Cremona, Mantova, Crete, Varese, Ampurias. The gulf of Lorraine. I know how to say 'I love you' in English, French, ancient Greek, modern Greek, German, a Celtic dialect, Dutch, Persian, Catalan, Turkish and Polish. Did she come alone?"

"I don't notice who my patrons come in with, as a matter of tact. The ruins in Genoa? Did you see the ruins in Genoa?"

"They are Peloponnesian. In Genoa there's only a cemetery. A port, a cemetery, brothels; it's an unbreakable order, always the same. Port, cemetery, brothels. Love, death, travel; they are stops along the way. Did she come alone? Did she ask for me?"

"That's not bad, that's not bad: brothels, cemeteries, ports. Recent arrivals would wind up either in the cemetery or in the brothels; that's probably the way it was. I don't talk with my patrons, especially women. Is the wine in Genoa good?"

"I didn't drink wine. I was in training. Genoa, Siena, Avignon, Brussels, San Sebastian. Did she leave any message for me?"

"I don't accept messages from my patrons, especially women. How do you say 'I love you' in German?"

"Ich liebe dich."

"London, Saragossa, Berlin. I would have liked to have been there."

"I wasn't. Where can I find her?"

"I don't know. I really don't know. Your father was happy about the trip. He mentioned a labyrinth and a tower. A basketball tournament and your Italian friends. Did you eat well in Italy?"

"Salerno, Oslo, Amsterdam. If she comes, tell her to wait for me. That I never left. I'm going to look for her."

He went out into the dark street with his ears ringing like on the basketball court. He was rebounding in Salonica; he was making baskets in Luxembourg. The night was dark in Berlin, rose and ochre in Madrid, damp and silent in Santiago, and he thought he could hear the shouts from the crowd in Genoa. The ball sailed at him. "Dai, dai." I love you. He went up in the air, as if pushed by the wind. "Dai, dai." Cars passed by quickly under the orange mercury lights of the Pont Neuf tunnel. "Dai, dai." And the ball came out of his hands gently (as if he were kneading, weighing something else—something sweeter, whiter, silkier than the ball) and went through the air ("I love you"), flexible, swift. She would surely prefer the surface of things, the chestnut trees ("marronniers," he sighed to a passer-by who asked for a light) of the Fustenberg plaza with its wooden benches ("Je t'aime," he carved with a knife point so that she could read it when she sat down) and their rounded dragon's feet. The ball fell cleanly through the net. The crowd applauded the shot. The tunnel under the Pont Neuf was empty. Neither his father nor his trainer would find them in the tunnel. On a bridge of yellow garlands and sandwich stands where together they would look for a print of a Monet evening. On a bridge, cold as a tunnel, in a tunnel dark as the night when he got lost in Offenbach after having taken the wrong bus and only knew how to say in German:

"Ich liebe dich."

The Bridge

ONE HUNDRED YEARS have gone by since the foundation
stone was set and the bridge inaugurated. Some may think this
too long a time, and truly this seems to be so, but only if one is
unaware of the details of the construction, the complex working
out of designs, as well as the material and spiritual obstacles that
stood in the path of its completion.

The bridge was first conceived one hundred and fifty years
ago as a way to unite two distant shores and facilitate communication between both sides of the river. I should say that even
if the river is only a fair-sized one, it still is the subject of much
pride among the citizens of the city, who otherwise would have
no river at all.

As any alert traveler or reader has been able to observe, the
most important cities of the world are built on the shores of a
river, in the same way that pedigree dogs are known for their
dark palates and fine paper for its watermark. Just like our little
city, London, Paris, New York, Amsterdam and Venice are traversed by a river, which doubtlessly distinguishes us from cities
more grand and powerful that don't have the flow of water to
reflect their palaces or industrial waste. Thanks to our navigable
river we have been included in numerous tourist guidebooks
even though we lack the usual luxury restaurants, gothic cathe-
drals or praiseworthy racetracks. (Long ago fish were abundant
on our coasts and pike would be jumping at noon, drunk with
the light. On the other shore, faraway oak forests stretched to
the sky as if hoisted up by the clouds. The current carried along

floating islands of water hyacinths, like small boats boarded by tadpoles, or the occasional snake pushed along by the current.) The river was our greatest pride and, without doubt, attracted many visitors who otherwise wouldn't have entered the narrow streets of our city nor rented rooms overlooking the river in summer, when the green water is as still as a swamp and swarms of insects are transported by the perfume of the wisteria.

Such has been our pride in our river that, since olden times, both shores have competed for travelers as if we were really rival cities. Those of us who live on this side of the river are convinced we have the best riverbanks, the most subtle shades of green, the most varied and abundant vegetation, the most delicious fruit and the best-planned civic harmony. The other side, with its foggy outline, might as well be another country: a place of high mists and sparse mountains whose inhabitants don't see the sun and who live in strange houses apparently made out of air. The river produces its own mist where it widens and disappears— much farther away than our eyes can see—into the oak forests where the owl lets loose its mysterious cry. But those on the other side take pride in their monuments, their marble avenues, their town squares hanging in the damp air, and assert that in the mist that rises from the river there are mysterious shapes, unknown birds and rare essences.

Maybe it was this hostility that first hindered the idea of a bridge, but as soon as our most prestigious architect (who was born on this side of the river no matter what those on the other side say) developed the project, it was accepted enthusiastically by the entire city.

It's true that work was delayed by an unfortunate dispute over which end was to go up first. Two antagonistic political groups formed (this happened more than a hundred years ago), and the dispute continued for such a long time that another architect, a rival of the first, soon appeared with a second bridge design which the administration studied for another few years. To be fair, and to calm agitated nerves, it was decided to build two bridges, one begun on our shore, the other on the opposite side.

Nevertheless, not everybody liked this solution. It was rumored that the second bridge (on the opposite shore) was better supplied; its materials were said to be more resilient, and its width a bit greater than that planned for our side, so the dispute started up again, this time with even more vehemence. Construction was delayed on both sides for quite a long time. The first architect died; a scarcity of raw materials forced on us a period of public austerity; many businesses closed and factories weren't selling their products. Somehow all this seemed to influence our thinking, and finally, we agreed to build only one bridge, which would begin on our shore. The bridge would end on the opposite bank, so our neighbors would have no complaints.

The foundation stone was set a hundred years ago, in a public ceremony attended by all the most important authorities. On such a solemn occasion, the inhabitants of both sides came together, as befits good neighbors. The minister read an eloquent speech, and the mayor took the opportunity to campaign for his reelection.

The foundation stone was large. It was hauled to shore by several city employees. But it was also docile; it stayed there many years without moving, bearing up under all the inclemencies of weather. We used to visit it often, especially in the early years when it retained its original character. The inclement summer sun slowly transformed its color until it resembled beach sand, while the autumn rains polished it into a mirror for small insects and a shelter for minute vegetation.

As the years passed, its size shrank and its loneliness increased. Almost nobody remembered that it was a foundation stone. Little children carved it with their knives, someone painted an obscene picture on it and, on one stormy day, lightning cut it in two.

The political maneuvers are obscure. A short time later, the rival mayor (from the other side of the river), a retired general who loved hens and monuments, decided to build the bridge beginning, this time, on his own side, and gave the task to a young engineer who had studied at West Point.

The foundation stone of this bridge was set eighty years ago. It was more square than the other stone and suitably dark colored. Several officials took responsibility for moving it, and when the wooden box was opened on the ground, the Municipal Band let loose with the city's hymn, the mayor read his speech and the Literary Prize was handed to the poet who celebrated the start of work on the new bridge with his verse (rhyming, of course, since he was an enemy of the avant garde).

Nevertheless, times were hard. The budget that the Central Administration had set aside for construction of the bridge was given over to improvements of our tanks and military equipment, because, as the general assured us, we should be well supplied to face any unexpected foreign assault. Moreover, the general asked for a special new budget, in case it was we who had to attack. The engineer emigrated to the United States, under contract to a university with a large budget, and a rare plague besieged our harvests. The stone, square as it was, was not to everybody's liking, and soon its defects were discovered.

One morning after a bad storm we learned that the foundation stone had disappeared. The river, which had risen, had taken it away at night along with trees and dead animals. This hypothesis, by all means plausible, did not satisfy everyone. Sure enough, some days later when the water settled back into the river bed, and the citizens affected by the flood began patiently to rebuild their houses, a rumor began to circulate that the foundation stone had not been washed away at all, as we had naïvely assumed, but rather had been kidnapped by the rival party. Groups of self-proclaimed "official citizens" began to comb the city—both sides—in search of it. After patient effort they found it, in fact, hidden in the depths of a cemetery on our side. We were immediately accused of kidnapping. While the long judicial investigation commenced—the extent and complexity of our manner of coexistence requires a long and meticulous examination of every issue—the rival party won the elections and the new mayor (a fair young man whose worst fear was to offend), tried to calm nerves by announcing that he would dedicate the next months to analyzing the problem, and afterwards would make a final decision.

Meanwhile the stone remained in the cemetery—dark, immobile and oddly square amidst the oval headstones.

After a year, our new mayor issued his statement on the subject:

"I didn't take it," he said, "and I didn't order its return. Therefore I won't put it back and I won't take it away."

Since then, alternate groups of citizens have taken it upon themselves to move the stone. Some agreed to meet in the cemetery and, protected by the dark of night, managed to drag the great stone to the shore. Thus, the next morning when we looked out at the soft curves of our shoreline, we saw rise up majestic and dignified the dark lump that one day would become the much longed for bridge. The water lapped serenely at its base, covered it with roots and then departed. The days passed and it remained there like a watchful beacon in the sea. But one morning we discovered that the stone had disappeared again; the shore was bare. The previous night, a rival group (aided by the darkness of a moonless night) had managed to take possession of the stone and keep it hidden away.

For days on end we looked at the smooth outline of the riverbank, desolate, without a sign of the stone. Some couples nevertheless continued to plan assignations "by the foundation stone"; if no one could be certain that the stone would be there in the evening, everyone knew where it ought to have been.

For years the stone motivated quarrels that put the city's peace in danger. Moved a million times, placed and dislodged from its spot every few days, it was the origin of dark revenges and violent reprisals.

The bridge was finally donated by a distinguished ambassador to whom we had given our vote for an international cause. Most amiably, he sent us a prefabricated bridge, extendible from shore to shore and rustproof to boot. Its inauguration coincided with our city's anniversary and we displayed it amidst a general celebration, despite our rivals' insistence that it looked like plastic. Our most famous folk singer performed old tunes in the popular spirit, and at night, spotlights illuminated the lacy mesh on either side of the bridge. The only problem is that we still haven't named the bridge. Several groups have formed to defend rival suggestions. Some insist it should bear the name of the first architect; others support that of the mayor under whom work began; there are those who defend the name of the old general, and others hint that, out of gratitude, it should bear the name of the ambassador who gave it to us.

The clashes are violent. There are groups who propose to boycott the bridge if it is not baptized to their liking, and the most radical propose acts of sabotage. The military, meanwhile, is on alert. It has no intention of tolerating any disturbances, and a special team of dynamite specialists are ready to act quickly. They'll blow the bridge up.

Atlas

HE HOLDS THE WHOLE WORLD on his shoulders. This shouldn't surprise anyone, since the world has lost its balance so many times. To hold the world on one's shoulders is an absorbing and delicate task that takes all his concentration; he can't allow himself any distractions, breaks, strolls around the lake or pleasure trips. He can't undertake any other task either (he can't have an interesting job in public administration or climb the entrepreneurial ladder); he hasn't looked for a wife and he doesn't have children. So, too, it's a silent and lackluster task, which explains why he doesn't get congratulatory messages at the end of the year, a Christmas bonus or any special prizes. People don't much seem to notice him holding the world on his shoulders, just as they don't notice the attendant in the public toilet; both know that theirs are invisible but necessary jobs.

He didn't always hold the world on his shoulders; the early years of his childhood passed without this responsibility, but they didn't last long; he has a hazy impression of that time, perhaps because the burden of holding up the world has ruined his memory.

He doesn't complain that it is he, and not someone else, who is holding up the world; he accepts it naturally, perhaps because he's a fatalist who doesn't believe in the possibility of substantially altering things. He focuses on his job although sometimes he wishes he could go for a walk or take a nice vacation.

He doesn't discuss the nature of his work with anyone, and he'd like for those who might see him holding the heavy world on his shoulders to give him a smile. But when this doesn't happen (and in fact, it doesn't happen) he doesn't get depressed. He's been able to adopt a wise indifference to worldly pleasures (which would be forbidden to him anyway by the nature of his work): comfort, luxury and the enthusiasms of the flesh. He has no religion, and he doesn't give his work any spiritual meaning; he'd hate to be the source of any religious or political craze.

Now that his health is declining (he is a mortal being just like everyone else), he wonders who will be called upon to replace him. He has no descendants and, anyway, he doesn't think his is a hereditary position. Nor does he think that the selection should depend upon any kind of social, intellectual or political merit. He knows that it's a burdensome, thankless and badly paid job—and the only one that can't be turned down. He doesn't know who his predecessors were and possibly he will be forbidden to meet his successor. But, perhaps due to his age, he remembers with special affection the little boy who one day began to hold the world on his shoulders. He doesn't pass any judgment on those men and women who, exempted from this task, turn to other employment.

What really bothers him is not going to the movies.

Guilt

HE HAS MADE A MISTAKE—but he doesn't know exactly what. In any case, this omission (his ignorance of the nature of his offense) only increases his guilt, for it attributes to him an element of stubbornness that is out of character. He would gladly repent, but he has forgotten his transgression so completely that he can't perform an act of contrition to prove his repentance and enable him to hope for absolution.

The worst thing about not knowing what he did is that he can't measure the consequences of his transgression; many events that occur in the world could be tied to it, but he'd never know. Horrible wars that scourge the universe, a child falling from a balcony, a woman raped or an old person freezing to death in a doorway, the extinction of the blue whale, the decline of film and the popularity of occult sciences—all might be linked to his transgression. Even though his transgression may have caused so many catastrophes, he is unable to stop them, since he doesn't know what he did (or did not do) to make them happen. When he watches television or reads a newspaper, something tells him that he has some hidden responsibility for the world's horrors. His offense is so embedded in his unconscious that he lives in apparent innocence; he finds out about the consequences like a foreigner reading the paper. An uneasiness arises. He has never been an Israeli soldier in Beirut, nor a North American in Vietnam; he doesn't traffic in drugs, nor has he killed anyone; he's not a fanatic, nor is he violent. He has a broad religious tolerance that verges on indifference. Of these he is sure he is not guilty. His offense must be of another order, one hidden from the vast majority, since he manages to hide it even from himself. Like a geological fault produced during the Holocene period, his offense (no matter when it occurred) has changed the world, unleashed an uninterrupted series of events, then rapidly closed in on itself, preventing him from knowing anything about it. Does the chestnut tree on a street in Montevideo know its origin? Since then his offense has not stopped producing certain effects, but he is completely ignorant of them.

He dreams often. He has wanted to look for information in the world of dreams, but his are dull, and he finds that if their fragile hypotheses confirm his guilt, they do nothing to clear up the mystery of its origin. Sometimes he dreams that in his student days he forgot to hand in an exam, in spite of which he still managed to graduate. One day he is discovered and he has to make amends; nevertheless all this time has gone by without anyone detecting his wrongdoing—not even himself—and now it's too late to lighten the consequences. Another time it is his task to feed a little white purebred dog (in another dream), and after several days he realizes that he has forgotten his responsibility: the animal has died, and he can't repair the damage. But what these and other dreams have in common is that there is always a double guilt: the offense he has committed inadvertently and the forgetting of it. And sometimes it seems to him that the latter is more important than the former; were the offense not disclosed, he could live unpunished forever, and the consequences would multiply into infinity, catastrophe after catastrophe.

Sometimes it occurs to him that he has actually broken a law he doesn't know about. Possibly not a human law (he knows these well), but rather a law of another kind: the secret law of the universe, inaccessible and not yet revealed. Perhaps, inadvertently, he has meddled in the higher workings, and his interference continues still, causing him to drag around this diffuse guilty feeling forever. Now, ignorance is no excuse when you're talking about either human laws or laws of the universe; so he can't justify his innocence, even if he can his forgetfulness.

He's convinced that the only solution is to be discovered. He needs someone to inform on him, to accuse him; he must appear finally before the people as a offender. Then, at least, he could defend himself. But he has pretended so well all these years that it is unlikely someone will appear who is willing to expose him.

The Trip

AFTER SEARCHING THROUGH OLD DICTIONARIES, several guidebooks with dark covers, ancient and modern maps, he decided on the city of Malibur—among other reasons because the most reliable data (from an encyclopedia consulted in the reading room of the National Library) indicated that around 1950 Malibur was inhabited by some sixty thousand people, a number that seemed to him very reasonable. Even if the citizens of the city had reproduced in a most enthusiastic way in recent years (which was doubtful; the books all referred to their common sense), they would never have managed to turn the city into the kind of crowded hodgepodge he found so hostile and unpleasant.

He got excited once his choice was made. He had taken a long time to make up his mind; it was extremely important to him to make an informed and clear decision about the city he would visit, and he would have never forgiven himself any carelessness or frivolity in the matter. First, he bought a world map that he hung on the wall at eye level. He secured the map with thumbtacks and, when it was finally spread out, felt the same dizziness that had come over him on other occasions (when he saw a beehive in buzzing frenzy projected on a movie screen, and when he touched thousands of burning grains of sand).

It was the first time he saw the entire world spread before his eyes: different cities with their complicated and difficult-to-pronounce names (indicated by black dots that looked like stop signs on an endless road), blue highways crisscrossing back and forth, and green threads of rivers unraveling or fading from view like wavy hairs. Without doubt, the world was a complex and diverse place, even though each individual imagined his or her town at its center.

He would spend long hours sitting on the sofa in front of his map, trying to decipher the secrets of routes, mountain ranges, lakes, historical or religious monuments, museums. To imagine each centimeter of the map multiplied to match the scope of the real world was just too exhausting and dangerous. Once, as a little boy looking at the night sky, he had tried to calculate the distance of a star and, in so doing, had gotten very dizzy. He stayed a long time staring up at the sky without hearing a sound; he left his world, the metal fence painted white, and had the sensation of floating in a silent universe illuminated by sparks of brightness and intense phosphorescent light. His mother had to call him several times before he answered, and the sounds of his name seemed strange; what was truly strange was to have a name at all and to answer to it, to identify oneself in any way and to recognize oneself as a being apart.

He had a similar response to looking at the world map, although this fascination had nothing to do with distance but rather with simultaneity: studying it he was able to confirm without question the coexistence of Louvain and Rij, Lamia and Pattrai, Fleusburg and Kiel, Portland and Norfolk, Catania and Ragusa, Vancouver and Glenora, Trieste and Bolzano. But his imagination disappeared into the infinite (that is, the void) when he focused on the immensity of the world living simultaneously at any given hour of the day, warm or freezing; and the imagination's limits, most assuredly, were a barrier to complete knowledge, to spiritual understanding; to be unable to grasp— due to a defect or weakness of the mind—the totality of the universe in one synchronized, but nonetheless diverse, image was probably the cause of many errors in judgment and deed in the tiny parts of the world that were ours to know.

He had already figured out the map's legend and therefore could distinguish principal routes from secondary ones, mountainous areas from plains, regions dedicated to agriculture from those known to be oil fields. Sometimes he filled lagoons with ducks, imagined a band playing on a podium in Quebec, built an amusement park at the exit of a highway, and meandered through an ancient cloister in a church set in a small medieval village.

He had told his friends about his plans to travel. The news was received with enthusiasm and no small envy. Everyone, in his youth or later on, dreamed about a trip, but no one had been able to take one. Money problems (so severe in recent years), family obligations, and work demands had made it impossible. The idea of a trip, postponed each time due to these material obstacles, lay deep inside each person, but at the same time these obstacles, shared by all, had created a kind of complicity, a solidarity in powerlessness and failure. If they had traveled, they would have gone to Paris, Florence, London, Amsterdam or Brugge; only the boldest would propose New York—just as in ancient times, facing a dragon was proof of the greatest courage. When someone in the café circle said, "I'd go to New York," he created a stir of admiration. Although the trip would never happen (and there were very few doubts about this), the mere statement of purpose was considered proof of daring.

When he announced his intent to travel, his friends celebrated the news with applause. First off, they ordered another round of drinks (they didn't let him pay, telling him he had to save for the trip) and started to argue about the preliminaries. Although no one had mentioned a precise date for the event, there seemed to be an unstated agreement that, even though there was no real hurry, it was necessary to get busy planning for the trip right away and not leave anything to chance or the inspiration of the moment.

He understood that the idea of the trip excited them and, even if he put it off for a long time, they all would feel obligated to help. Moreover he realized they all hoped the trip would take place as far into the future as possible so they could plan to their hearts' content.

From this day on, their gatherings at the café became more lively, and nobody missed a single one. They wanted to protect him; for he had given them a pastime that alleviated their routine, pain, and daily humiliations. The trip turned into their only topic of conversation; each made it his own, pouring on recommendations, initiatives, and suggestions without expecting him to follow their advice. Everyone worried about his passport. As a matter of fact, like the majority of citizens, he didn't have this document—which seemed like a bad joke or a clear symbol of failure to those who knew they'd never travel—and moreover cost a lot of money.

The easiest and fastest way to get one was discussed in great detail. One friend remembered that he had a cousin in the Administration; the cousin was well connected, so it was decided to ask for his most estimable help in a country of civil servants whose bureaucracy was as defective as it was prestigious. Another friend knew a photographer with ties to the police who could take as many photographs as necessary to please the official at the Registry office.

One uncertainty, which no one mentioned out of tact, was the trip's destination. In truth, it didn't seem important. Now that he had received an inheritance and could actually make the trip, everyone realized it was travel that was important, not the destination. Nevertheless, when they all got together on winter nights in the old café with its wood furniture and chipped mirrors, what was important to them—penniless men, exhausted from family problems and repetitive, poorly paid jobs, who were never going to travel—was the trip's destination. So, when one of them announced, "I'd prefer to go to Paris and then, maybe, to Limoges," a long discussion would ensue. Someone would suggest that Paris was not what it used to be; the center of European culture had moved, and Vienna, the birthplace of psychoanalysis, offered far more excitement than the land of Rimbaud. French thought had dried up—perhaps only Lacan in recent years had renewed it—and the absence of poetry was the most significant sign of this deterioration.

If someone else proposed London, he was immediately challenged by the others. It didn't make sense to choose London today, since English culture, so excessively self-absorbed, had lost all its vigor (that lucidity and clarity of thought that had characterized all the followers of Swift); at best, London could manufacture musical groups, athletes and young people with hair tinted green.

Although nobody doubted the beauty of Venice, it was an embalmed beauty, sold in its rags to tourists, consumed by avid North American senior citizens and photographed far too often.

Montreal was interesting only for its purple mountains in autumn, but who would travel so far just to look at trees?

Discussions of this sort consumed the friends' late nights. He participated too, although always with the sensation that something unknown was escaping him.

Just two months after he announced the trip, somebody got the idea to ask without much ado as if it were an unimportant issue: "Have you thought of where you'd like to go?"

By that time, the cousin in charge of the passport had got him to sign the initial paperwork, and an appointment with the photographer had been made.

He confessed that he had not yet decided where he would travel. They took the news without alarm, but with understanding. Surprisingly, they were quite tactful about this point.

"One has to think things over before making a decision," someone thought out loud.

"Absolutely," said another, "one can't travel to just any old place."

"What's important," added a third, "is to have made up one's mind. The place, that's the least important. The world is full of places to go."

"The cities aren't going anywhere," advised the fellow to his left. "There'll always be a London and Paris. No reason to get nervous."

Meanwhile (as he passed his days dedicated to the contemplation of his map, as fascinated as if he gazed into a fish tank with electric lights and orange fish), they took care of other tasks that had nothing to do with selecting a city, but which they considered to be as necessary and even more urgent.

One took it upon himself to put together a comparative schedule of time differences among all the major cities in the world. This allowed him to know, without ever getting up from the sofa in front of the wall where the world map was hanging, what time it was simultaneously in Moscow, Lisbon, Herzegovina, Naples, San Francisco, Munich, Tokyo, Baden-Baden, Cali, Marrakech and Guadeloupe.

He got used to thinking about cities by calculating in great detail what time day would break in Stockholm and when evening would fall in Casablanca. Sometimes he entertained himself with visions of a woman taking her dog out for a walk in Manhattan while the milkman delivered bottles in Liege or a girl rode her bicycle in Kreuzberg.

Another friend supplied him with a list of jazz records that, according to a 1970 catalogue, he could buy in Soho—records, moreover, that were unobtainable in their city.

Alejandro wrote down the names of the most important museums in the world, indicating the works in each one that, in his opinion, had to be seen.

The more practical Irineo worried about foreign exchange, making sure he knew the rates and pointing out the importance of the black market whenever there was one.

Pablo furnished a list of the most famous brothels in the world and the special services they provided according to an international guidebook he had obtained.

Santiago made up a list of indispensable items that ought to be in a suitcase, no matter what the destination of the traveler or the season of the year, on which appeared among other things: a multilingual dictionary of common phrases, razor blades, a hand calculator, a toothbrush case, two tortoise-shell—unbreakable—combs, airmail envelopes (there was no reason to lose time trying to figure out what they were called in German or Swedish), a scarf, a card with first aid instructions, and a good luck charm, whatever kind one liked.

Sometimes the friends argued among themselves in the café about some concrete detail related to the trip (how many rail lines left Frankfurt, or the capacity of the port of Lisbon, the pollution rate in Barcelona or the quality of wine in Padua) while completely ignoring him, as if the trip were really something happening to them all, and not just to one person. He even got into bitter quarrels with some over such things as the size of the Berlin racetrack, the food given to pigs in Rijvaj, the existence of madrone trees in Madrid and pollution in the port of Marseilles. Alejandro assured him that only in Russia was the air pure, since factories there had a special system for getting rid of toxic emissions, and Pablo recommended that he not drink the water in Naples if he wanted to avoid an ulcer.

While his friends spent their time designing his trip, he acquired guidebooks and dictionaries for the delicate task of selecting a destination. He didn't want the selection to be given over to chance nor inspired by those widespread prejudices about countries and cities, based as much on climate as on customs, on food as on national character. He would pick out a city on the world map on his wall and then consult the encyclopedia. Other times, he proceeded the opposite way; he would open the dictionary to any page and when he saw the name of a city, he would go look for it on the map. And so he learned about cities that have disappeared, that no longer exist and whose names have changed repeatedly. (One night he thought he had fallen in love with the city of Abitur in the Baltic, destroyed by crumbling icebergs two centuries ago. He wanted to become familiar with its frozen palaces, columns of lapis lazuli, bridges of glass, the crystal mosaics on its walls. He wanted to walk through streets enveloped in thick fog that, in the distance, outlined the shapes of lost ships, of imaginary animals with the heads of parrots and the feet of dogs. He wanted to meet its women, transparent and slender as vases, who strummed strange metal instruments and chewed a substance that kept their lips unharmed in spite of the cold. But the city no longer existed. He imagined a journey in his dreams and woke up with the unpleasant sensation of having returned unwillingly, just as sometimes we leave without wanting to do so.)

He didn't make known the nature of his inquiries, and he had a vague sense that the selected city would not be one that his friends were considering or even could imagine.

Some cities were eliminated for their dense populations; others were rejected because they didn't have rivers or lakes to release thought and encourage memory to flow. Neither did he want to travel to a city enclosed between mountains, because he was convinced that the mountain inhabitant had a closed spirit, lacked horizons and was by necessity provincial. He disdained cities that had no forests because the eyes and soul need green in order to rest.

After six months of vacillation, he chose the city of Malibur. According to a guidebook with a hard blue cover that he had bought at a fair, it was a small city of medieval origins, traversed by a river, in a wooded valley full of ash, oak, and carob trees. Malibur was the fourth or fifth (historians don't agree) city built on the spot, and excavations had revealed the pyramidal structure of the second city, the fortress-like wall of the first stratum and the piles remaining from ancient huts of the third (a period in which, after a shift in land, a lake was formed). It had a Gothic cathedral, an old bridge watched over by two lions, a ceramics museum, a collection of optical instruments, and a train station with an old iron structure that looked like a lizard's skeleton. The guidebook offered some historical information and recalled that, some centuries ago, the inhabitants were known for their beautiful weaving; however, it didn't say what the present occupation of Malabarians might be.

One day at the end of November (November days are melancholy and the daylight takes on copper tones), he told his friends of his decision to travel to Malibur. The news was received with jubilation. He hadn't yet set the date, but Irineo reminded him that it was important to make his reservations early. There was only one travel agency in the city; its posters had faded over time, and the only agent whiled away the day with crossword puzzles from the newspaper, or engaged in endless hands of solitaire on a wooden table with old brochures whose timetables were no longer accurate.

"From now on, you will go to bed earlier," Antonio decided.

All agreed.

"The best way to prepare for a trip," proclaimed Irineo, "is to keep regular hours and good discipline. You have to eat at the right time, go to bed early and not commit any excess."

Although he didn't know what kind of excesses he could commit in this place, he was pleased to think that he didn't engage in them because of his preparations for the trip rather than for lack of opportunity.

Pablo gave him a box of aspirin to keep in his suitcase because they might be necessary at any moment, and one never can tell when a headache will come on. Santiago opened a box made out of newspaper; inside was a pair of thick woolen socks knitted by his mother, an industrious and resolute old woman who fed him and told him what shirts to wear. Alejandro presented him with a bottle of cologne because it's good to splash on before bed after a long day of walking; Irineo, with great ceremony, presented him with an old black belt with an opening in the middle, just right to safeguard one's money. Irineo advised him to use it even when he was naked.

The friends spent some weeks studying possible methods of transportation to Malibur. Although at first he didn't have any inclination to fly (he didn't like to be strapped down, he was afraid of getting airsick, and he detested the idea of not seeing the landscape), a cruise was eliminated, since the boat went to a port from which it was possible to get to Malibur only once a year, and the friends were afraid that on the day it set off he would be sick, would forget his hand luggage or would arrive late to the dock, which would require him to wait another full year for the next boat.

Once the method of travel was decided (it would be air, then bus, inasmuch as Malibur didn't have an airport), he convened all his friends and, with great ceremony, informed them of his decision to study the language of Malibur, since the best gesture of goodwill that a traveler can make on arriving at an unknown city is to speak the language of its inhabitants. They all agreed with this plan; moreover, they decided that in order to take full advantage of his time, he would be excused from the nightly gathering in the café. So, he could dedicate his nights to learning a new language while they, gathered in the bar, would discuss additional preparations for the trip.

From what he could find out, in Malibur they spoke a Celtic dialect, scarcely used beyond their borders, called Malabar. Although very few people in the world know the basic grammar and vocabulary of this language, the text that he consulted—an old history book written a century ago—revealed that each inhabitant of Malibur spoke it in a different way, that they were very proud of their dialect—it wasn't wise to call it that in public—and that they scorned foreigners who spoke to them in another language.

He didn't find a single Malabarian grammar, and the only dictionary he could find was Celtic, but it included some dialectical variations in the margins, among them those used in Malibur.

Supplied with a notebook and pencil, he began to study the language of the city he was going to visit. His friends had been right to excuse him from their gatherings at the café; he soon learned that the solitary study of a language was an extremely complex activity, full of rough going, of ambushes-in-waiting behind the apparent simplicity of the phrases; and, while one word led to the next, it was true, still the road was bristling with difficulties. So he learned that it was useless to try to know a language if one knew little of the history of the people who spoke it, but in order to learn this history reasonably well, one needed a basic background in geography, zoology, and botany. The study of a language couldn't be separated from the study of the economy, arts and sciences of the people who used it, and especially not from their technology: it was as necessary to know the manner of making shoes as the declensions.

For many months his friends devoted themselves to amassing all kinds of information and documents to inform the traveler about the civilization and history of the Celts, knowledge without which it was impossible to study Malabar. But since there wasn't much material, he decided to move permanently to the reading room at the National Library and not to leave except to go home to sleep.

He would jot down his discoveries and revelations in a notebook.

After a laborious analysis (he had to do a comparative study of a text in French and in Celtic), he discovered that the word *gwan* = soul and the discovery filled him with joy. That night he went to meet his friends with the light and satisfied heart of one who has been graced with revelation and feels touched by its divine aura.

Gwan meant soul and surely *kells* was "heart" (he felt inspired just walking down the street, and the traffic lights glowed in a friendly way—nice little guys with leaden feet) and he thought that from these two or three words, others would spring forth like a waterfall, hurrying to reach his mouth and be caressed by his tongue, that he would savor them like fruits from an as yet unknown tree. And so *tropzell* had to be "skip," because the *kells* gave a *tropzell* in the *gwan* when one was about to discover something one loved. (Regarding genders, the old hard-cover dictionary explained that the Malabarian dialect recognized around twenty-three, having to do not only with the sex attributed to objects but also with other information no less valuable: there was a gender for warm things and another for cold ones;

a gender for round objects, for square and triangular ones too; a gender was assigned to youth, another to adulthood and two for old age—which really did surprise him; finally there seemed to be a wide range of genders for emotions which were classified according to their intensity.

When he announced that he had figured out some words in the Malabarian dialect all by himself, he was warmly congratulated by his friends, who raised their glasses in unison to toast his achievement.

"Tomorrow we'll go to the travel agency," declared Irineo. "It's time to make reservations; it's important to do these things well in advance."

Everybody agreed, and they didn't let him pay that night; instead they presented him with a list, in writing, of the things he was to get for them during his trip.

Alejandro wanted a photograph of a Druid altar—he hoped that one was still left in Malibur—and a pebble fallen down from the rocky coast.

Santiago asked for a natural silk scarf; if Malibur was a city once known for its homespun goods, he supposed that some still remained.

Pablo wanted a bottle of water from a public fountain because, according to Celtic tradition, water from public fountains, applied to cellular tissue, was a preventive against loss of virility.

Irineo wanted a set of bookplates from the oldest printing press in town.

The next day they all went together to the only travel agency in the city. Due to the scarcity of work, it opened only a few hours each day. The agent, a young man, had an air of self-assurance: he wore a black tie over a striped shirt and had long yellowing fingernails. On his desk were a deck of cards blackened with grime, a dried-up inkwell, a bronze ash tray in the form of an airplane, and two barely used rubber ink pads. On the wall were three blurred posters: one, faded and stained by damp spots, depicted the steps of a Roman circus. Another was of the ski season in the Ardennes; the skier had jumped from quite a height, but the paper under his feet was torn so that he appeared to be lost in the air, like an astronaut thrown from his spaceship. The third was an island scene, presumably in the Caribbean; the palm trees were faded, and the water, because of the deteriorating paper, looked like land.

When they told him of their intention to buy an airline ticket, the agent looked at them with a cynical and disdainful smirk. They felt vaguely uncomfortable. The man went through the motions with a slowness and indifference that Alejandro judged to be offensive. He moved the ash tray to the edge of the desk, shuffled some useless papers that were put away to one side, submerged his fountain pen into an obviously dry ink bottle and then held the pen to the light as if he were very interested in examining something through it.

"You can always judge a guy by his work," Irineo proclaimed out loud. The agent placed his pen on the desk, turned slowly and stared off in Irineo's direction, but without focusing. Now he seemed to have gone into a kind of automaton dream state, but this was less disagreeable than before. Finally, he extracted from a deep drawer a thick book with yellow pages. It looked like an old telephone book, and they felt somewhat nervous, as if its pages contained something threatening, a judgment or a veto written long ago that was now lying in wait for them.

The young man pulled over a bench from the back and, cocksure, began to write. He set a long printed sheet in front of their eyes and finally said, looking at the traveler with a pompous air:

"When do you want to travel?"

He thought. He thought about the dictionaries that covered the table in his house and that still hid dozens of facts; about the cryptic and brilliant phrases that seemed about to jump out at him to reveal their deepest meaning; about the twists and turns of a language slowly uncovering its secrets, but only if he, for his part, tried to know the history of Malibur, its geography, its way of thinking, its ways of firing pottery and of roasting its food, its warring and weaving, its system for creating analogies from memory and its technology of glass making, its manner of love-making and curing illness, its ways of celebrating holidays and burying the dead.

"Within three years," he answered. "I think I'll be ready to travel by then."

Some Research on the City of Malibur

Malibur's currency is the *tropel*. On one side of its coins is depicted Katia, the only woman in Malibur to display royal dignity, and on the other is an orange peel, the exchange unit before money, with which all transactions were made. Following is a list of market prices at the time:

1 pig = 15 orange peels
1 cow = 14 orange peels
1 cauliflower = 1 orange peel
1 suede coat = 7 orange peels
1 virgin woman = 6 orange peels
1 non-virgin woman (good for farming) = 2 orange peels
10 kilos of flour = 5 orange peels
10 liters of wine = 2 orange peels
1 Ullrich painting (the most famous painter in Malibur)
    landscape = 2 orange peels
    portrait = 3 orange peels

For many years it was required to wear a hat in Malibur, in public as well as in private. The Prime Minister was bald and tended towards feelings of inferiority.

The word "birds" (*akerós*) was forbidden because of an infestation of birds that scourged the countryside and ruined the harvests for two years in a row. The Minister of Agriculture took this measure to combat them in the most efficient way, convinced as he was that only that which can be named is real. Expelling them from language, he hoped to drive them away from the land. When the Malabarians wanted to refer to them without mentioning the forbidden word, they used to say "the silent archers" or "comets with tails" or "scourge of the land."

Malabrians refuse to build monuments or to fulfill their military service.

The city's animal is the dinosaur "because it has back feet in the past and its head crosses into the future."

Malabarian grammar has only one verb tense, the present, since "the past is a dream and the future a nostalgia."

Private property was severely assailed by Magnus Millus, the most important Malabarian philosopher (1562–1608) who considered it to be proof of selfishness and stupidity. Millus' influence was very significant and is still seen today in the language: possessive adjectives are not used except in the case of "my death."

The telephone is rigorously controlled: it can be used only to call the doctor, firemen, veterinarian, dentist, police or Town Hall. Thanks to this measure, there is an active social life in Malibur; people visit one another, meet in plazas and cafés, go to concerts and plays.

There are no political parties in Malibur because politics are not considered an art or a science, a trade or a profession. Every four years a public lottery is held (in the presence of a clerk), and citizens selected at random take over the tasks necessary for the administration of public office.

Malibur does not have an army, navy or air force. But it does have luxuriant forests.

The diet of the people of Malibur is based on seaweed.

The three years passed quickly, faster than he would have liked. At the end of this time he met with his friends and told them of his decision to postpone the trip.

"I am still in the preliminaries of my study," he said to make a long story short. Studying the language had brought him imperceptibly to the study of philosophy which he could not responsibly undertake without some familiarity with related fields. ("All of them," he summarized, very concerned with saving time). From there he had moved to studying technology—of crafts as much as of industry—and then to art. But Malibur was not a closed-off valley floating autonomously in space, and he had no other choice but to study the relationship between its culture and civilization and those of others, from other places.

"I'm at a crossroads," he confessed to his friends, and the word seemed very appropriate because it was the name poets give to turning points in a road and he was just about to make a journey.

At this moment his major concern was to find out what influence *The Characters* by Teofrastus had exerted on the *Ethics* of Mark Allen, founder of Malabarian philosophy whose works were read in all the schools; but he had still not been able to find a single copy of the book. So as not to disappoint his friends, he gave them some good news: he had learned how to prepare the major desserts in the Malabarian cuisine, all made out of seaweed. They all celebrated the news, and he invited them to dinner on Saturday and promised a meal, right from a Malabarian cookbook, that he praised as healthy and delicious.

For the next two years he tried in vain to have some communication with an inhabitant of Malibur; by now he knew the language sufficiently well to write a few lines expressing his many doubts, sometimes about the city's geography, other times about its zoo and many more about the details of its history. They began to think that Malabarians were unsociable and uncommunicative and that they probably rejected foreigners. But Alejandro—more of a realist than the others—thought that the letters had never gotten to Malibur. The postal service in the country where they lived left much to be desired, and it was most probable that letters—the few that the naïve still left at the post office—were stuffed, forgotten, in some drawer or tossed into a mildewed bag thrown into the basement of some branch office.

During this time Irineo got married and stopped going to the nightly gatherings at the café; he had to spend his nights writing horse racing reports for a daily paper in order to increase his earnings. He only came on Saturdays and then asked:

"Are there racetracks in Malibur?"

The traveler kept them punctually informed of his new knowledge about the life, history and customs of the city although, due to his scrupulous sense of duty, he also told them of his doubts and uncertainties. There were philosophical concepts he couldn't grasp, and Malabarian literature gave him some difficulties that weren't going to be easily resolved.

Meanwhile Santiago had contracted the painful disease of melancholy (very common among inhabitants of the place) and also stopped going to the gatherings. He would spend his nights holed up in his room, mute, staring at a fixed point on the immovable wall. Even so, the last time he uttered a word was to say to him:

"Send me a postcard from Malibur."

His fortune decreased (inflation made as many inroads as melancholy), but he wasn't unduly worried; he had other things to think about. For instance, what was the origin of the goddess Kali, omnipresent in ancient Malabarian myth, but also adored in India under the name of Durga, symbol of knowledge and invincibility?

In the fall of the second year Pablo was arrested for some unclear conflict with a colonel; the prison discipline was so severe that he couldn't have visitors. Nevertheless, he managed to get a written message to them once. It said, "I'd also like to learn Malabarian. Send me your notes."

Before the second year was up, Alejandro moved to a town in the interior of the country. He had gotten a job as telegraph operator in a train station and had to live in a house nearby, but he was happy because he didn't have to pay rent. Before saying good-bye, he told him, "This trip is not like yours. You can't view the sea from this town and there's not a lake either. Think of me when you're in Malibur.

He ended up alone in the city, so alone that sometimes he wanted to talk with one of the employees at the National Library, but these fellows were only interested in soccer and the lottery. When he finally discovered the relationship between some anthropomorphological images from Malibur and the Indian cult of Siva, he wrote a long letter to Pablo, thinking that, stuck there in jail, he would enjoy sharing this secret pleasure. "But my conclusions are not definitive," said the letter. "It will be necessary to check them against Parker's studies on the mythology of Yanaon. I've just ordered the book through Minerva Bookstore. It will take at least three months to get here, with luck. I expect to spend about six months reading the book, then six more comparing his conclusions with mine. For this reason, I've postponed the trip for another year and a half, a reasonable time to finish my studies in this area."

Eighteen months later, on a warm and sunny April morning, he silently pushed open the glass door of the only travel agency in town. The door gently reflected his image. He was dressed in his best clothes, and he gave a look around to make sure that, indeed, nothing had changed in the last six and a half years. The agent was the same (but now he had grown a little dark mustache, as was the fashion) and the posters too. The same skier had made a leap into the void, and the Caribbean island seemed as faded as ever.

The agent surely recognized him (he hadn't changed either, just like everything else in this city that was falling apart ever so slowly) and although he made no effort to acknowledge him, their eyes met. Afterwards the agent's indifferent eyes returned to the newspaper, opened to the crossword puzzle. "Indian divinity. Five letters. Female," he muttered to himself.

"Durga," he responded without any hurry.

"Oh, yes?" responded the agent, as if it weren't anything important at all. But he wrote the word down, and it fit. Then he looked at him calmly. "What would you like?" the agent asked him finally.

He slowly plunged his hand into the inner pocket of his sports coat. It was a well-tailored Prince of Wales that made this agent with the yellow fingernails a bit envious. His passport, brand-new, with its bright blue covers, clean and unscratched, stuck out from a leather wallet. Next to it a thick wad of bills was arranged in order, with the figure of the Liberator on one side. On seeing the long salmon-colored bills, the agent closed the newspaper and looked attentively at his client's hands. The posters on the wall hung there like dirty laundry, and the agent promised himself he'd change them. A yellowish light edged with lilac strips filtered through the windows. The weather was like that; it changed all of a sudden. It was the only thing in the city that varied in any way.

The agent waited for him to speak. Far away a thunderclap rumbled.

"I want five posters of the city of Malibur," he stated at last, slowly and firmly. "Big and in color," he added. "Order them. I don't care how long it takes. Nor how much it costs."

As he left the agency, the first drops of rain began to fall. The store lights were on, and he took refuge in a doorway; the rain always excited him, and he enjoyed observing the reflections of neon lights on the wet asphalt. While he was waiting for it to clear up, he thought that night he'd have to try out a recipe very famous in Malibur. Sliced seaweed with rice.

Patriotism

THE CITY HAS TWO FLAGS, one red and one black. They aren't solid red and black; the red one has a black lion embroidered in the middle, and the black one has a red eagle in the upper left corner. No one is certain where these symbols came from or what they mean, nor does anyone recall the origin of the flags, although the rivalry between the Redflaggers and Blackflaggers is so intense that wars and rebellions are frequently arranged between the followers of each group. You see, whenever the Redflaggers take over (whether through free or fixed elections, military coups or foreign intervention) they immediately decide to ban black flags from all flag poles and buildings in the city, just as when the Blackflaggers run the government (by whatever method they can), they forbid the red flag.

Redflaggers and Blackflaggers are irreconcilable, bitter enemies, although on second thought, it is very hard to explain the differences between them other than the color of their flags and the presence of a lion on one and an eagle on the other. It's true that in parades, for instance, followers of the red flag disguise themselves as lions and followers of the black flag dress like eagles; it's also true that patrician families like to call young Blackflaggers *eaglets* and newborn Redflaggers *kings of the jungle*. But aside from these differences in names and symbols, it is difficult to find the true differences between the two. Nevertheless, nobody freely chooses to be a Blackflagger or a Redflagger; it's a hereditary tradition that one receives at the moment of baptism. The Blackflaggers, just like the Redflaggers, remain so

57

for their entire lives. Of course, there are always traitors: a daughter quarreling with her parents who, in a rebellious gesture, decides to abandon the Redflag cause and cross over to the Blackflaggers; a husband divorcing his wife (all marriages take place within the group) who embraces the flag of his wife's enemies. But these are rare cases. Both the Redflaggers and the Blackflaggers look on converts with distaste; they don't try to convince but rather to defeat.

The symbols used on both flags are even stranger when you consider that there have never been lions or eagles in this city (there are no jungles or thick mountain forests, and the land all around the city is completely flat), so any power the figures may have comes from drawings or stories from other lands. But the followers of the red flag or the black flag don't ponder these questions; they care only for action.

Frequently, their deeds are heroic. When the Redflaggers are governing, for instance, a Blackflagger will assault the city's central tower, tear down the red flag with his bare hands and raise up the black flag. He's almost always knocked off by some well-aimed shots from army guns, but for a few moments he manages to see his standard wave in the bell tower.

One of the public ceremonies most esteemed by both groups is the burning of flags. It's like this: several followers of the banned flag get together and, in the center of the plaza, spray gasoline on the despised official flag and set it on fire while they roar like lions (if they are Redflaggers) or caw like eagles (if they are Blackflaggers). A big crowd gathers and the ceremony is made good use of by vendors of sweets, cotton candy, peanuts, pennants and balloons. Beggars ask for money and people set off firecrackers. *Flag burning* (by either side) has become a national holiday although an attempt to regulate it through a series of decrees put forth by Blackflag congressmen has never succeeded, since it is a legislative tradition in this city never to pass a decree sponsored by the opposition, be it Red or Black.

When a very old Blackflagger is near death, he asks that his coffin be wrapped in the beloved flag lest his bones never arrive at their final resting place. In spite of the risks (if the Redflaggers are in power), the family tries to fulfill the final wishes of the dead man, celebrating the funeral with the prohibited banner on top of the coffin. But the Redflaggers (or the Blackflaggers, as the case may be) always find out, and then there are violent confrontations, with new victims. The next day there are even more funerals in the city, some with red flags and others with black ones.

Redflaggers and Blackflaggers divide up the cemetery, too. For nothing in the world would they have their dead intermingle; then the dead would have to be avenged by their descendants, as it is stated on building walls and in proclamations.

If a foreigner passing through (Redflaggers say they don't like foreigners and Blackflaggers proclaim to love them, but this is only a rhetorical dispute: what is clear is that neither group likes foreigners) tries to find out the reasons for the century-long hatred between the groups, he or she will hear an identical litany of similar wrongs, all related to the color of the flag, the form, the possibility of exhibiting it or not in public ceremonies, the eagle or lion costume and the superiority of one over the other in the animal kingdom.

Artists and scientists also take part in this squabble. So Redflag writers publish their works under such pseudonyms as Leon Heroic, Leo King or Leonard Good, whereas Blackflag actresses always show off their filed artificial nails, use creams to brighten their eyes and wear long black capes that cover their bodies.

Men of science spend many hours investigating the physical characteristics of the lion, its habits and customs, and claim (if they are Redflaggers) its supremacy among the animals, while Blackflag scientists, convinced of the superiority of the eagle, have determined the capacity of its flight, its orbit, the time it spends in the air and the details of its sexuality. Many supplementary symbols are on display in the city's store: mirrors with an engraved lion or eagle, coasters, bottles in the shape of a lion or eagle, badges, charms, ashtrays, matches and lamps. Car motors are usually painted red or black just like the fronts of houses. All of which shows the high level of patriotism that exists in the city.

Gratitude is Insatiable

A MAN DID A FAVOR for my father once. He gave my father directions after he had gotten lost in a city he didn't know very well; and not only this, he also went along with him for a bit to make sure he didn't make any wrong turns. My father was moved by this act of generosity, and every time he told the story (and he told it very often, too often), he couldn't keep the tears from his eyes; it was the first time in his life that someone had done him a favor, and he was determined never to forget it. When they said good-bye, my father promised he would never cease to be grateful.

Although we were poor, my father managed to put together enough money to buy a box of candy and send it to his benefactor. A little later he sent him a lottery ticket that didn't end up winning. Distressed by the passing of time, which did little to lessen his sense of indebtedness, my father decided to set a date each month on which to send a gift to his benefactor. At this rate he sent fountain pens, decorated almanacs, glass tigers and deer, porcelain ash trays, a compass, a sailor's cap, a piece of dry coral, a bronze lamp, a cigarette box, an illustration from a book, suitable for framing, a book by an English philosopher, several cans of tea and a hand warmer used by German soldiers in the Second World War.

Concerned about repaying his debt, my father worked a little more each day and added other dates for sending gifts to express his gratitude; now he also sent candy and cigarettes on Christmas, Easter Sunday, and St. Christopher's Day, his benefactor's patron saint. All of us were aware of this debt of gratitude, and we all contributed to the best of our abilities so that our father could repay his debtor.

Gratitude is insatiable, so an English minister and philosopher assures us: instead of being paid back, a debt increases and we can never work enough to cancel it. My poor father was continually moved by his memory of the favor he had received, and every day he added new details that increased his feelings of gratitude and his tears as he thought about his benefactor's kind gesture. So we learned that the man had advised my father how to get to his destination even though it was nine o'clock in the morning (an inappropriate time to take a walk since everybody else was going off to work), that the weather had been somewhat cold and large storm clouds had glided by in the distance. Moreover, the benefactor went some meters out of his way to accompany my father, which possibly made him lose some precious minutes of his valuable life and made him miss the bus that took him daily to the office where he worked. This isn't all either: he also made him a drawing on a piece of paper showing exactly what my father should do to get where he was going.

Gratitude is anxious, affirms the same English reverend and philosopher: the smallest doubt about one's feeling of gratitude increases the debt. Two years after receiving his favor, my father contracted an incurable disease; having been separated by hospital walls from the world of the healthy, and by a coma from the world of the living, my father woke up to learn that this unexpected mishap of nature had made him forget about the gifts he was to send, and he was overwhelmed with anxiety and guilt.

During the two years that had gone by since the moment my father received help, his benefactor made no attempt to respond or keep in touch, but when my father woke up from his deep coma, horrified to learn that he had let the habitual date of his gifts go by, he asked us insistently to call and convey his deepest apologies. My father's eyes filled with tears when he realized the full extent of his oversight.

As a matter of fact, the benefactor had noticed the absence of his habitual gifts, he told us on the phone, and kindly accepted our apologies. We assured him that, whatever our father's health, this wouldn't happen again and he seemed satisfied with our promise.

My father was overcome with happiness to know that his benefactor forgave his offense and immediately gathered together his scarce resources and ordered us to buy a leather cigarette case, which we very quickly sent with a card reiterating my father's eternal gratitude.

True gratitude is inexhaustible: it is bottomless, observes the English reverend and philosopher. The more one tries to settle a debt, the more it increases in geometric proportion to the favor one believes to have received. My father had not fixed a date for the debt to expire, and he understood that the debts one wishes to repay (as opposed to those never to be repaid) are never wiped out, but he accepted this like a gentleman because he feared that his benefactor would think he was forgetful of the favor he had received.

Before he died, my poor father had us all assemble around his bed and told us of his wishes for the disposition of our inheritance. In truth, apart from some personal objects still in good condition (like his shaving brush, a refillable fountain pen, a pocket watch with a gold case, four pairs of socks, glasses for the near-sighted, his glass ink well and some photographs from his youth), my father had very little to leave us, except his debt. So he told us:

"My children, you have observed that during the last years of my life, I have taken great care not to forget my benefactor, and

I have attempted to carry out the obligations that gratitude has demanded of me. Gratitude is eternal; this passion has consumed my life. I implore you and I order you to continue my work, and in my name, to accept the debt I leave you as your only inheritance, with the awareness that you are fulfilling a debt that has been so dear to me."

In fact the debt had been costly, and from that moment on, if we accepted our father's bequest, we were very careful not to deserve any other favor.

The Nature of Love

A MAN LOVES A WOMAN because he believes she is superior. In truth, this man's love is based on his awareness of the woman's superiority because he couldn't love an inferior being nor one who was his equal. But she also loves *him*, and if this pleases and fulfills some of his dreams, it also creates great uncertainty for him. In effect, if she is really superior to him, she can't love him, because he is her inferior. Either she is lying when she says that she loves him, or she is not superior to him, for which reason his own love for her cannot be but an error of judgment.

This doubt makes him suspicious and torments him. He no longer trusts his first impressions (about the beauty, moral rectitude and intelligence of the woman), and sometimes he accuses his imagination of having invented a nonexistent creature. Nevertheless, he has not made a mistake; she is beautiful, wise and tolerant, superior to him. She can't, therefore, love him; her love is a lie. Yet if this is really the case, if she is really a liar, a faker, then she can't be superior to him, a man distinguished for his sincerity. Her inferiority thus proven, it is not fitting that he should love her and, nevertheless, he is in love with her.

Disconsolate, the man decides to separate from the woman for an indefinite period of time; he has to clarify his feelings. The woman apparently accepts his decision as a matter of course, a fact that again plunges him into doubt: either she is a superior being who has understood his doubts and said nothing, in which case his love is justified and he should run to her and ask forgiveness, or she didn't love him, which is why she can accept the separation with indifference, and he shouldn't return to her.

In the town where he has withdrawn, the man spends his nights playing chess by himself or with the life-sized doll he has just purchased.

The Parable of Desire

AFTER MANY DECADES and over several generations, we finally were able to fulfill our desire. This common desire, shared by all the inhabitants of the city, gave us our character and imprinted unmistakable traits on our identity. (We were quite careful to expel those who didn't share it, excluding them from public life, persecuting them with our contempt until they were driven into madness—or to the border.)

It was this desire that distinguished us from others, encouraging us in moments of anguish and forcing us to withstand the vicissitudes of daily life. We recognized one another from our desire, passed on from parent to child like the curve of a nose or the color of hair. During our inevitable but frequent trips abroad, we were able to gather in strange cities thanks to this tenacious desire, imprinted on our memory like a secret stamp.

For a long time the majority of our civic acts, and our private ones as well, were aimed at obtaining the object of our desire. There were some victims, of course, because desire intensifies with obstacles in its path and grows larger with pain. Our victims filled a gallery, were preserved in memory and on the walls of buildings. But the fulfillment of desire was always in the future and this brightened our days.

Finally we attained it. Like someone who climbs a massive and winding mountain path to the peak. Like someone in a labyrinth who spies an exit. Like someone who discovers water in a desert well.

At first the fulfillment of our desire filled us with joy. We left the intimacy of our homes—where desire lived hidden among the old stones, water stains and ceiling moldings—and turned out into the streets to celebrate. We were all family and friends. We forgot past offenses, ill-will and envy. Normally closed, our doors were opened without fear. We drank and we sang. We festooned the balconies with garlands, the avenues with flowers, and we plucked, once again, instruments that had been put away in attics. We paraded through the streets, gave impassioned speeches and paid homage to all of those who suffered the pain of dying without having reached the happiness of desire fulfilled.

Now sadness has followed euphoria. The streets are empty and faces are lifeless. No one sings, and domestic quarrels continue one after the other, petty and cruel. Moreover, public arguments have begun. Some maintain that *this* was not exactly what we desired, and they insist that our desire was perverted the moment it was fulfilled. But the oldest among us turn to the ancient chronicles, records, and poetry to prove the origin of our desire. Others go only so far as to insinuate that perhaps we haven't interpreted our tradition correctly or that our desire has changed, slowly but treacherously, over time. No matter, these arguments do nothing to revive our spirits. The weariness brought about by a desire fulfilled sometimes hides animosity. A young man without scruples (whom we punished, as he well deserved) went so far as to proclaim in the city plaza that the fulfillment of desire is lethal, and that our error was to try to fulfill desire rather than to prolong our longing. Worse yet, he said that it was not a mistake in the objective of our desire (as some had come to think) but a misunderstanding of its profound nature, which consists in defying fulfillment. He added that we had cheated our young people, depriving them of an inherited desire that they suckled from their mothers' breasts, one that they shared, like the color of their skin, and that freed them, moreover, from the painful anxieties of an individual desire worked out over nights of insomnia and madness.

Relaxed and empty of our desire, we wander through the streets like people who have lost something. We barely say hello (such is our lack of vitality), and if the desire was once a cause for zeal and communication, its satisfaction and its last stage (possibly eternal), listlessness, has made us solitary, introverted and unlikely to join together in a common cause. Now that we have fulfilled our desire we no longer have enemies to unite against. Since no one opposes the desire, we have no reason to get together.

Some cautiously suggest that perhaps we should devise another desire, but the suggestion falls into the motionless void of our will, of our spirit. The satisfaction of our former desire has left us without imagination and without faith. Like the dry earth after a flood, nothing can grow out of our satiety. Even a fool knows that the fulfillment of desire is usually called the *end* of it, a word that in almost all languages also means conclusion, death, termination, and that this coincidence should have warned us about the nature of satisfaction, but we paid no attention since we are almost deaf and blind. We are creatures without a future because we no longer know how to desire.

The Revelation

HE WOKE UP AT THREE IN THE MORNING, terribly excited. He usually dreamed very little, but this time, unlike others, the dream came to him with absolute clarity and the images stayed sharp, and he was without that sense of disorientation that we usually have when we have woken up trying to remember our last dream without betraying it. The message was strong and simple; it left no room for confusion. The image of the Lord had given him an order with a clear and sure voice: "Abandon everything and go out into the streets to preach the truth." There was no doubt that these were the words and, in the dream, he bowed spontaneously and submissively, feeling a great happiness, a sentiment of humble joy; it seemed that finally he had given in to an order without uncertainty; his mission stripped him of all the insignificant things he had spent his life doing, showing him the only transcendent one. So that when he awoke, he was still feeling the strange happiness of a man who believes that he has understood.

He got up immediately—it would have seemed lowly and contemptible to stay in bed—and turned on the light. It didn't matter to him that it was night and that the house lay in a silence of darkness broken only by far away sounds: cars still crossing the avenue, a siren from an ambulance, and a dog barking in an apartment. Even with the lamp on, the dream retained its initial sharpness.

He got dressed quickly because there was no time to lose. What most excited him about the dream was that it significantly

altered his sense of time. Because he had an urgent and press-
ing mission to accomplish, the minutes and seconds took on
another dimension, a moral character, that had been missing
from his life since adolescence. He wasn't an indifferent person,
but the morality he lived by he had invented for himself without anybody's demanding it of him. Until this moment he had
been both judge and defendant within this moral code; now his
mission tied him to a superior order before which he felt sub-
servient; now he couldn't judge, only defend.

The light woke up his wife, who looked at him curiously. He
was a rather methodical man, and he didn't usually get up at
three o'clock in the morning, nor did he walk around the room
in excitement at this hour.

He hesitated a moment. He didn't know if he should tell his
wife about his dream. On the one hand, his emotions spilled
over onto others; his happiness was generous; but on the other
hand, he thought that the intimate nature of his revelation, its
truth undemonstratable except through an act of faith, made it
impossible to share.

He was not a religious man. His contact with the Church
had ended when he was still a child, the very day those other
more urgent and pleasurable, but ambiguous, contacts became
known to him. It had seemed to him that having sex precluded
having a church, and he concluded that any negotiation between
them was contemptible. Since then he hadn't given a thought to
religion. Now, as he was looking anxiously for a suit in his closet,
he thought that sex was not at all important and that the years
he had left to live would hardly be sufficient to obey the order
adequately. Joy filled his heart with enthusiasm and propelled
him onward. The room seemed too narrow to hold him back,
and for a moment he thought he could jump from the window
into the street without getting hurt. He restrained himself

sufficiently to realize that he couldn't risk the mission for a stupid accident. What suit should he put on? They all seemed inadequate. He thought that perhaps one of his wife's plain and loose-fitting tunics would be best, but he hated to stand out, and he didn't want to be taken for a lunatic or an eccentric. He felt a secret repugnance toward the blue suit he wore at the office, contaminated as it was by little everyday worries, inane conversations and resentments. As for the bottle-green tweed, it had a superficial and elegant quality that now looked brazen. His sportswear seemed frivolous; then he remembered an old black suit from his youth that he had refused to throw out for sentimental reasons, and he rescued it from the old trunk where, amidst out-of-style shoes and hand-knitted scarves, it was calmly being eaten by moths. He shook it out a little to knock off the dust, examined it under the lamp; it seemed a bit shiny around the knees and the lapels, but he knew intuitively that it was just right. While he was putting it on, it seemed that his mental and emotional excitement was almost impossible to keep in check. He would go out to the city center and he would immediately begin to preach; he thought with joy that the revelation was going to free him from his office routine, uncomfortable visits to relatives, small domestic squabbles, weekly sports pools, excursions to the countryside, bottlenecks on the highway, annual visits to the doctor, and taxes. It was going to free him, too, from his secret pleasures: the Friday visit to a certain attractive and by no means prudish lady, the retrospectives of old movies at the film club and the chess game with a bright but boring colleague. He felt light and stripped of all cares. He didn't judge his previous life, up to the day of the revelation; surely a man who has not been touched by grace is a man innocent of any guilt, and he wouldn't be judged by his actions prior to this moment. From now on, on the other hand, he was excused from the responsibility of choice because his mission was obligatory and didn't leave any room for doubt: other things were merely supplemental, and there was no confusion about them: anything that wasn't the mission ceased to exist.

Encased in his black suit—which he found surprisingly comfortable after all this time—he set out for the bus stop. He checked the schedule on the metal sign and realized that he was going to have to wait a good long time. It didn't matter; enflamed by passion, he grew suddenly enormously tolerant of the insignificant problems of city life. He didn't bother to develop a method of preaching; just as the force of revelation in his dream convinced him immediately, so too he thought it would suffice to tell the story, to evoke the gray yet luminous sky in which God had appeared so that he who wanted to hear would understand, and he who did not could leave the path. In truth, the order he received was to preach, not to try to convert. A black cat passed quickly by his side at the bus stop, and he had a desire to stop it, pick it up, and caress it. But it fled rapidly. The street was deserted under the half light given off by mercury street lamps, and the immobility of the cars parked on the pavement and the sounds of the traffic lights changing colors gave the city an unreal look that he knew well. It was the absence of human beings that created this atmosphere, like a landscape after a war. Like a city made of glass, thick in the night and motionless, where no one lives any longer.

When he got on the bus, he had a doubt: it seemed to him that the image of the gray sky where the Lord had appeared was no longer the image from the dream but rather the memory—during his waking hours—of the dream. This sensation depressed him suddenly, and he tried to recover the first image without any of the changes that memory might make. He closed his eyes in the effort. The bus was empty, and he had settled into a seat on the street side. It seemed to him that the black man outside was identical to the one in his eyes when he closed them. In this dense darkness the little figure of God now appeared with difficulty and, what was worse, His face had taken on a ridiculous grimace that in no way resembled the expression in the dream. He became irritated with himself, with memory's deception. Where had he gotten that expression that was super-imposed on the original image? Surely it was a remnant of another face that, like an expressionist drawing, adhered to the original, deforming it. He fought the collage, trying to return each face to its original contours. He didn't have any success. The new face of God, deformed into a cartoon-like grimace, was the only one that would come to him; this grotesque image was the only one he could summon. When he opened his eyes, he surprised his own face in the window, and he observed that the effort had furrowed his brow. It wasn't the only thing that had changed. In the dream the Lord had gestured before speak-ing to him. Now, as much as he tried, he couldn't recall the ges-ture. Had He parted the clouds? He wasn't sure. Suddenly the gesture of the Lord parting the clouds formed in his head but he couldn't figure out if it was the image from the dream or one that his imagination had made up later. Which was the original? He thought that the gesture of parting the clouds was a little child-ish; maybe it came from some drawing he saw as a boy, rather than from his dream. He cursed himself, because in his emotion after waking up, he was not able to fix in stone or in metal the authentic image he had dreamed of. Anguished, he repeated the order he had heard while sleeping. "Abandon everything and go out into the street to preach the truth." In the first place, he should be sure what kind of God had spoken. From what he knew, there were numerous gods and some rejected the others. His conscience, nevertheless, reproached him right away. Wasn't he looking for an excuse to get out of his assignment? And if this were true, if in truth he was trying to escape from his task, what event had pushed him to change his will? When he went down into the street, he had no doubt that he wanted to fulfill his mission. What was the part of himself that now was trying to elude it? To reinforce the command, he tried to remember his dream again, but now the images he managed to evoke were faded, comical or blurred. The Lord—whoever He was—parted clouds in a grumpy way, and one of them, as round as a balloon, was slipping away down the side of a mountain. This seemed like a stupid detail that in no way could belong to the original dream. The landscape that had surrounded the appearance of the Lord now seemed really naïve. Nevertheless, as far as he could remember, when he awoke he had found it to be effective, clear and revealing. It was not that an extravagant or spectacular setting was required, but the empty plateau he had dreamed about, with its dark cypresses to one side, its gray sky with clouds made of golden filaments, was just too conventional. This is the way the pupils from the religious school had painted it during his childhood. Why would the Lord have made use of such a naïve structure?

He got off the bus at the end of its run without knowing very well what to do. The oral message still resounded in his ears, but now a few details seemed necessary. It wasn't enough just to station himself in the middle of the main plaza and recount the dream. What was the truth he was supposed to tell? He wasn't willing to play the pathetic role of those small-time mystics with their long dirty hair and worn-out, torn tunics, who went around murmuring unintelligible things to passers-by and who were given some coin out of pity. Insofar as abandoning everything, fine, yes, but did that also include the visits to the attractive and by no means prudish lady? There was no reason to explain his new mission to her; he was sure that it would be difficult to convince her of any metaphysical truth, and she would certainly write him off as a lunatic.

He went into one of the few cafés open at this time of the morning and asked for a chamomile tea. The waiter answered that they only served alcoholic beverages, and then he hesitated. Could he ask for a cognac? Did his mission forbid drinking? He decided one cognac wouldn't betray his orders. While he was drinking, in little sips, he saw himself in the long and narrow mirror on the wall, and the black suit seemed anachronistic. More than a man touched by divine grace, he looked like a country bumpkin just off the train and lost in the city. He was a rather shy man, and he asked himself why the Lord would have selected him, considering the trouble he had starting a conversation or approaching a stranger. For him to do so, the revelation would have to have an extraordinary force, and now when he recalled it, it got lost among gray clouds that rolled around like balloons on the side of the mountain, and the Lord's strong presence—endowed with an outlandish expression—seemed like that of a ham actor in a corn ball comedy.

He drank three cognacs and left the place. He got to the office early, convinced that he had missed his one opportunity to free himself. He didn't tell anybody about his failure because he knew that, on telling it, something of the old command would shake him, and he was unwilling to look guilty in the eyes of other people. His guilt was a secret between the Lord and himself. Surely he could put forth as an extenuating circumstance the fact that his memory was unfaithful, his evocations unclear and his imagination treacherous, but he was sure these justifications were weak and wouldn't mitigate his sentence. His joy was reduced to the modest conviction that he had been illuminated once, but the infidelity was that of his own abilities, much more than his will or his disposition; certainly, it would have been absurd to follow the instructions of a God whom he remembered topped off with a ridiculous expression and who parted clouds that looked like balloons.

When he recalls the revelation, he tries to strip it of images (images that his memory had deformed and transformed into caricatures). But he knows that time goes by with a morality that he can no longer separate from his conscience, and if he still keeps going to the office, playing chess, making bets and visiting the attractive and by no means prudish lady, he does so on two levels: on one he carries out his daily activities as if nothing has happened. On the other, he knows that he is irremediably lost and that nothing he does can be worthy of justification. Sometimes he puts on a black suit and goes out into the street in hopes of finding someone who will listen to the story of his dream without asking uncomfortable questions, but if he finds this person, he stops: the parody of the dream has already happened in his imagination, and the greatest betrayal he might commit takes place in language.

Final Judgment

THE MORNING NEWSPAPERS didn't announce an eclipse, and the forecast promised good weather, clear skies and little humidity; thus, in principle, there was no reasonable explanation for the presence of a large violet cloud advancing sluggishly toward the mountain like an unseemly presence, an unplanned indiscretion of the sky.

He wasn't willing to hasten his step—no matter that the soft breeze of September might become a wind, as it seemed quite ready to do—because he was a man of solid principles, moderate political ideas and strong convictions; anyway, those leaves that were now whirling around his head were a subversion of September's order, and he decided not to pay them any attention. Nor was he willing to consider the purple color that the mountain had taken on, completely out of place if one takes into account the early hour of the day in which he was setting off, with measured pace, to his work in a bank office on one of the central streets of the city.

But this wasn't all. When he got to the corner—a cross street full of store windows where his profile blurred like a sort of far away mannequin—he felt a drop of rain on his nose, and he noted that a middle-aged lady who was going by in the opposite direction opened her umbrella like a medieval dome. It seemed humiliating to him.

And if this weren't enough, the vendor at the newsstand where he always bought his paper greeted him hurriedly, unfolding over the newspapers and magazines a piece of plastic that

87

fluttered in the wind like a trapped butterfly. "What strange weather!" he felt the obligation to say as he took money from his pocket to buy the newspaper.

He saw indistinct women's forms under dark yellow rain-coats. What he hated most about the brusque disappearance of the sun was that it altered, even confused conventional notions of time. In truth, the gray sky that was opening up now like a circus tent could be that of the early morning or mid-afternoon, and he detested uncertainties, confusions, vacillations.

He had to quicken his step against his will, which he considered a small personal indignity. It seemed that life was full of ordeals and disagreements impossible to repair.

The violet cloud spread out like an ink stain and covered the sky. The air had acquired a Prussian blue tone, and he was happy that this expression came into his head because in the uncertainty of this morning that seemed like an afternoon, it summoned up a sense of order even if it was a military order. But Prussia had gotten lost somewhere, sometime.

Then he heard the booming of thunder, hollow and charged with electricity, like an iceberg suddenly breaking up. He shuddered. Ever since he was a boy he couldn't keep from trembling violently whenever he heard that trombone in the sky. He was going to send a letter to the Meteorological Center. It wasn't acceptable for them to make this kind of error in the weather forecast. Didn't he pay taxes regularly? Didn't he go to work every day, arrive punctually and never take time off?

The second roar of thunder, even more spectacular than the first, caught him just as he was quickening his step to cross the street, and it boomed like a large building falling to pieces. Then a crash that he couldn't identify made him raise his head. It hadn't begun to rain consistently yet, but red and yellow lightning drew winding rivers in the sky like lines on the maps one got in school. These lightening flashes divided the sky in two, and the dark clouds parted like curtains rising on a stage. Behind them the landscape just coming into view was more serene (he seemed to pick out a small blue area, pure and with amber-colored borders.) The sky appeared to open up, submissive, to make way for another sky. And if everything was harsh, churned up, damp and electric in the superficial sky (the one closer to his eyes), the other, the one that appeared behind, was tame, radiated a harmonious light and, especially, was not a noisy, but rather a silent sky. It evoked the religious cards of his childhood, with their apocalyptic landscapes, lilac-colored clouds and light beams that went through mountains. Everything that he had rejected as childish in his maturity returned in this naïve vision like a joke in bad taste: it was the exact place where the old man reconciles himself with the boy. And he couldn't stop looking; for a period of time that he could never determine, he remained absolutely still, as if he had surprisingly lost the ability to move, and he thought that if anyone walked by at that moment (but now the street was strangely deserted; most probably the bad weather had cleared it out), he or she could have perfectly well taken him for a statue.

Then suddenly in the great opening in the sky, like a stage curtain going up, he saw God make his appearance. He didn't come down or make any movement; He simply appeared among the clouds, only His head, and both looked at one another for a moment.

Everything was motionless around him: he observed that the trees on the street were floating, the cars lay immobile, a sepulchral silence reigned on the street (you could only hear the rhythmic sounds of the traffic lights changing), the passers-by had disappeared, and the lilac light of the buildings made them seem to float like houses suddenly turned into boats, and he into

Noah. Surprisingly, he wasn't nervous; he felt comforted and at the same time vaguely disappointed. Comforted, because with everything resembling the religious cards of his childhood, a certain part of his uncertainty disappeared; and disappointed, because he couldn't stop thinking that, whatever else it meant, this vision was naïve.

Finally they found themselves face to face. This seemed to be the most important moment in his life, and everything since his birth brought him to this instant, this revelation, this culmination.

He tried to move but felt as if something or someone, without effort, were restraining him.

Then he spotted other people inside their houses, also motionless just as he was: speechless dark shadows, immobilized forever in the moment of lifting a fork to their mouths, opening a door, petting the cat, reading the paper, writing a letter. Like mechanical dolls suddenly halted by some flaw in the works or frozen by a child's wish. Even more, he thought that from the beginning, in the clear dawn of time when things were first named, everything had led to this in some mysterious but steady, obscure and inescapable way. Everything: Napoleon and the seven Infantes of Lara, the Medicis and Charlemagne, Etruscan cemeteries, Teutonic orders and slips of the tongue, paintings by Murillo, Hesiod and films by Chaplin, women who die in childbirth, the swans on the Wansee and the drawings by Utamaro, the Second World War, the music of Wagner and the martyrdom of Ursula, the October Revolution, the student rebellion in Cordova and the opera Evita, haiku, the Beatles and Eleanor of Aquitaine. Everything led to this, through the enigmatic paths that the short span of human life could never grasp, but that now were revealed in all their inevitability.

He was a cautious man, and the last day couldn't take him by surprise. He had remembered the Biblical verse that told the just

man to prepare himself for the great event; he didn't have anything to lose because he hadn't held on to anything, and the
trumpets of Jericho, thunderclaps though they were, resounded
in his ears like the echo of ancient music. He had awaited this
day anxiously, but also humbly and with meekness, because no
one should be so proud as to expect to be selected for the last
day. He had prepared himself silently, without harboring any
ideas about rights in the matter, and now he had his opportunity.

Finally they found themselves face to face. He dug around in
his pockets. Time had stopped, frozen like water in a lake.
While he was digging around in his pockets, he made a gesture
to God, asking Him to wait. What could an instant mean when
it comes to all eternity?

From the inner pocket of his jacket he took out some type-
written pages (he was a meticulous man), and putting on his
glasses (he suffered from a slight far-sightedness) he began to
read God a list of charges that for fifty years had accumulated
against Him, impartially, like an anonymous investigator who
has followed a suspect without His ever knowing.

A Moral Lesson

A GREAT STEP FORWARD in my moral development (self taught: my parents were atheists and so did not send me to any church, and nearsightedness kept me out of the army) was understanding that I shouldn't forgive my enemies even if they had not yet destroyed me. Moreover, to recognize that I *had* enemies was a beautiful moral lesson. I usually acted as if I didn't have enemies, and if this discouraged them somewhat, it was fundamentally due to my deep conviction that there was no reason at all for me to have any.

It was an absolutely beautiful day. In the morning I boldly recognized that my youthful appearance (in spite of my forty years of age) could cause envy in others and my lack of conceit could be interpreted as the most arrogant pride. I saw that I was compassionate with the dull-witted and, instead of encouraging them to be otherwise, I always tried to hide my intelligence, which surely earned me their contempt. I didn't flatter anyone, which provoked the hostility of those who wanted to be praised; I resisted the urge to compete for money, fame or power, and in so doing, I didn't allow myself the opportunity to triumph over others.

But this wasn't all. In the afternoon (a beautiful spring afternoon in which the air smelled of honeysuckle) I recognized that the worst thing was my stubborn refusal to acknowledge blows. If someone tried to hurt me, I immediately, and with great generosity, showed him that he had succeeded and extended my hand in friendship. Doubtless, this caused some bewilderment

and insecurity among my enemies, although in my moral confusion, I believed I didn't have any. Whenever anyone managed, after many attempts, to hurt me in any way, I hid the
damage from him and from myself, so that our apparent friendship could continue and my aggressor never know of his success.
Then, convinced of the failure of his earlier attempts, he would
feel obliged to repeat his attack.

I should confess that this behavior utterly confounded my
aggressors. An ancient law (that I, with my scanty moral development, did not know about) maintained that enemies must
recognize one another, respond to blows, and attack one another
mutually. But my permanent smile, the delicacy with which I
treated my aggressors, and even my confidence, gnawed at them
and moved them to hold grudges against me. Indeed, had I
deigned to acknowledge the hostility of their feelings or the
hurt I had received, they would have had the opportunity to present themselves as magnanimous, generous, even repentant;
possibly they wouldn't have attacked me again out of consider-
ation for my weakness and even would have offered me help. But
when they attacked, I pretended not to notice. I hid my wounds,
staunched the flow from my tissues in solitude and, the next day,
the enemy found no trace of his aggression. This displeased
him profoundly; he awaited reciprocity in our interactions, be
they friendly or hateful. To acknowledge that the aggression
had been ineffectual punctured his vanity, diminished his self-
esteem; my refusal to defend myself gave him guilt feelings, and
my continued offer of friendship seemed to him to be unequiv-
ocal proof of pride.

At night in a rapture of lucidity, I realized that I had accepted
envy disguised as love from my enemies; I had kissed traitors and
praised the reticence of the envious, transforming it into discre-
tion. That night before going to bed I understood something

else: to pardon our enemies if they don't want to be pardoned is an affront. It is the violation of the offender's intimate desire. By pardoning my enemies in the very moment they were trying to assault me, I robbed their acts of completeness and perverted them in two ways. On one hand, I prevented them from reaching their objectives; on the other, I robbed them of an authentic repentance, for if they hadn't committed any offense, as I made them think, instead of asking my forgiveness, they had to repeat their aggression. There is nothing worse than being forgiven for a offense that has not been committed. And this was what I did with my enemies.

After these reflections, which took me all day, I felt comforted. I had been able to overcome the pity that my enemies inspired and my natural tendency to forgive (a shameful defect in my character): now I was a moral being, just like my enemies.

The Threshold

THE WOMAN NEVER DREAMS and this makes her intensely miserable. She thinks that by not dreaming she is unaware of things about herself that dreams would surely give her. She doesn't have the door of dreams that opens every night to question the certainties of the day. Nor the door of dreams through which we enter into the past of the species, where once we were dinosaurs among the foliage, or stones in the torrent. She stays at the threshold, and the door is always closed, refusing her entrance. I tell her *that* in itself is a dream, a nightmare: to be in front of a door which will not open no matter how much we push at the latch or pound the knocker. But in truth, the door to that nightmare doesn't have a latch or a knocker; it is total surface, brown, high and smooth as a wall. Our blows strike a body without an echo.

"There's no such thing as a door without a key," she tells me, with the stubborn resistance of one who does not dream.

"There are in dreams," I tell her. In dreams, doors don't open, rivers run dry, mountains turn around in circles, telephones are made of stone, and we never get to our appointments on time. In dreams we don't have underwear to cover our nakedness, elevators stop in the middle of floors or smash against the roof, and when we go to the movies all the seats have their backs to the screen. Objects lose their functionality in dreams in order to become obstacles, or they have their own laws that we don't know anything about.

She thinks that the woman who does not dream is the enemy

97

of the waking woman because she robs her of parts of herself, takes away the wild excitement of revelation when we think we have discovered something that we didn't know before or that we had forgotten.

"A dream is a piece of writing," she says sadly, "a work that I don't know how to write and that makes me different from others, all the human beings and animals who dream."

She is like a tired traveler who stops at the threshold and stays there, stationary as a plant.

In order to console her, I tell her that perhaps she is too tired to cross through the doorway; maybe she spends so much time looking for her dreams before falling asleep that she doesn't see the images when they appear because her exhaustion has made her close those eyes that are inside of her eyes. When we sleep we have two pairs of eyes: the more superficial eyes, which are accustomed to seeing only the appearance of things and of dealing with light, and dream's eyes; when the former close, the latter open up. She is the traveler on a long trip who stops at the threshold, half dead with fatigue, and can no longer pass over to the other side or cross the river or the border because she has closed both pairs of eyes.

"I wish I could open them," she says simply.

Sometimes she asks me to tell her my dreams, and I know that later, in the privacy of her room with the light out, hiding like a little girl who is about to do something naughty, she'll try to dream my dream. But to dream someone else's dream is harder than writing someone else's story, and her failures fill her with irritation. She thinks I have a power that she doesn't have and this brings out her envy and bad humor. She'd like for my forehead to be a movie screen so that while I sleep, she could see all the images from my dreams reflected on it. If I smile or make a gesture of annoyance during the night, she wakes me up and

asks me—dissatisfied—what happy or sad thing has happened.
I can't always answer her accurately; dreams are made of such a
fragile material that often they disappear as soon as we wake up;
they flee to the eyes' web and the fingers' spiders. She thinks that
the world of dreams is an extra life that some of us have, and her
curiosity is only halfway satisfied when I am finished telling her
the last one. (To tell dreams is one of the most difficult arts; perhaps only Kafka was able to do so without spoiling their mystery, trivializing their symbols or making them rational.)

Just as children can't stand any slight change and love repetition, she insists that I tell her the same dream two or three
times, a tale full of people I don't know, strange forms, unreal
happenings on the road, and she becomes annoyed if in the
second version there are some elements that were not in the
first.

The one she likes best is the amniotic dream, the dream of
water. I am walking under a straight line that is above my head,
and everything underneath is clear water that doesn't make me
wet or have any weight; you don't see it or feel it, but you know
it is there. I am walking on a ground of damp sand, wearing a
white shirt and dark pants, and fish are swimming all around
me. I eat and drink under the water but I never swim or float
because the water is just like air, and I breathe it naturally. The
line above my head is the limit that I never cross, nor do I have
any interest in going beyond it.

"It's probably an old dream," I tell her. A dream from the
past, from our origins when we were still undecided about being
fish or humans.

She, in turn, would like to dream of flying, of slipping from
tree to tree way above the rooftops.

Sometimes while she sleeps I put a little pressure on her
forehead with my fingertips in order to bring on a dream. She

doesn't wake up, but she also doesn't dream. I tell her the last dream I had, of a prisoner in a small punishment cell, isolated from light, time, space, human voices, in an infinity of silence and darkness. There's a guard next to the door and the prisoner manages to inject—through the walls of the tunnel as through the membranes of a uterus—his dreams into the guard, who then can no longer rest, hounded as he is by the prisoner's dreams. The guard promises to free him if the man can frighten away the lion who hunts him down each time he dreams.

"You're the prisoner," she says with a vengeance.

Dreams are like boxes, there are other dreams inside them. Sometimes we happen to wake up in the second rather than the first, and this makes us anxious. In the second, I try to call her but she doesn't answer, she doesn't hear me; then I wake up and call her again. I open my arms to her, not knowing that I am in the first dream and that this time she will also not answer.

I propose that before falling asleep we have the experience of inventing a complementary story, the two of us together. Surely then some remains, castoffs, residue of this story elaborated by the two of us would pass imperceptibly to the inner part of our eyes (to the eyes that open when the superficial eyes close) and in this way, she would finally manage to dream.

"We'll take each other to the threshold," I tell her, "and when we get there we will separate, giving each other a kiss on the forehead, and each of us will go through the door—her and his door—and we'll meet again the next morning after a different journey. You'll talk to me of the tree you saw and I of the ship that takes me to the city I hope never to see again."

That night we go to bed at the usual time and I am the one in charge of beginning the story that is to take us imper-ceptibly—but together—to the auspicious door.

"There is a man in an empty room," I begin.

"The curtain is very soft," she says, "made of red velvet, but it is tied at one end."

"The man is lying in bed," I continue, "although he is still wearing the white shirt and the dark pants."

"I think the man is afraid of something," she continues. "That's why he is still dressed."

"Next to him is a woman," I say, "with short blond hair. Her eyes are blue."

"No," she corrects, "they are green with blue flecks."

"Yes," I accept. "She is beautiful, but she has the cold skin of those who do not dream."

"The woman has on a pink dress. Isn't it somewhat outmoded to wear a dress of this color to bed?"

"No, sweetheart," I say. "It looks great on you."

"He's just about to fall asleep," she observes.

"Yes," I confess. "I'm very sleepy. I am walking slowly towards a door that takes form up ahead."

"You are walking slowly with your shirt sleeves rolled up and your eyes half closed."

"I'm really sleepy."

"She's following you but every moment gets farther behind. Her steps are shorter than yours and, moreover, she's afraid of getting lost. Why don't you turn to look behind you, to help her?"

"He is very tired and the path is guiding him, pulling him like a magnet."

"It's the magnet of dreams," she says.

"The woman is very far behind. She can't be seen any longer. On the other hand, I am at the threshold."

"She's gotten lost again. The corridor is dark and the walls narrow. She is afraid. She is terrified of solitude."

"I've seen this threshold before."

"But I can't see it at all."

"If you go back, if you turn around, you'll never find it."

"I'm afraid."

"Ah! What an auspicious threshold! You can make out a light once you cross over."

"Don't leave me alone."

"There's not much space."

"Don't leave me."

"I have to go on. I'm at the end of the pathway, my eyes are closing, I can't talk any more…"

"Then," she continues, "she throws herself forward, following the vague and dark aura that his footsteps have made in the shadowy corridor, and before he crosses over the threshold, she plunges a knife in his back."

I stagger on the threshold, I fall like a wounded person slowly in the dream, it's strange, I slip, I collapse, now I have one foot over the threshold but the other one has stayed behind, it doesn't move forward, surely I am in the second dream although the pain in my back is possibly from the first, I'd like to call to her but I know from experience that she won't answer, she has probably gone while I try in vain to wake up and I slip in a pool of blood.

The Art of Loss

WHILE HE WAS WAITING HIS TURN at the dentist's office, the man read a two-page article in an illustrated magazine entitled "The Secret of Personal Identity."

He wasn't an assiduous reader; he only read to kill time, in the waiting room at the train station or the dentist's office. Every once in a while he would buy a sports newspaper or a news magazine, but in general he preferred television. Nevertheless, it seemed fitting to read in the doctor's waiting room or the barber's chair in order to avoid the temptation of staring at his neighbors' faces as well as to reduce the anxiety of waiting.

He read the article carefully. In it a psychologist from Anneversie Hospital in a small town in South Dakota asserted in a clear and categorical way that all men have a secret: the secret of their personal identity.

This revelation dazzled the patient, who was awaiting his turn in the somewhat rickety cretonne-covered chair (it was a neighborhood orthodontist who was having to fight increasing competition) and created an excitement that was hard to control. He went over the black shiny letters (the magazine used a coated paper) that were fleeing towards the edge of the page like ants; it was true, Mr. Irving Peele of Anneversie Hospital affirmed that all men (that meant him, too) had a secret, the secret of their identity, something that they could never reveal completely even if they wished to do so, and that they would take to their tombs without being able to convey even to their wives and children because it was something essentially inexpressible.

"I have a secret and nobody knows it," murmured the little man, all caught up in the excitement. He closed the magazine and looked on the cover for the date of publication. He discovered that it was a very old issue, dated two years earlier. At that time he was forty-eight years old and had half fallen in love with a girl he'd met in a park one afternoon when he didn't have much to do because unemployment had left his days free. If he had told her that he had a secret, that he possessed an intransmissible but true identity, maybe she would have shown more interest in him. At that time too his upper, second to right, molar was bothering him, but he wasn't ready for extra expenses, and anyway, going to the dentist was no fun. He preferred to go to bars with videos, to watch a show by Julie Andrews or Frank Sinatra, who sang for all generations like a somewhat obscene but immortal angel. How long had the magazine been sitting here, on the glass table in the office, with its revelation inside? Why didn't this news, of interest to the general public, appear on television? He could see Dr. Irving Peele on the screen explaining in detail that each man possessed a secret (perhaps women too, even if they were not spoken of specifically) even if he didn't know it; and maybe the girl would have wanted to get to know him, to search for his secret, the one he unknowingly possessed.

For the moment he closed the magazine and hid it under the others because he felt possessive about his discovery and thought that it was better that few people knew about it. To have a secret—even if he wasn't exactly sure what it was (didn't the psychologist say that it was something inexplicable?)—gave him a vague power even though he didn't yet know how to use it.

He thought about pulling out the two pages to read in the privacy of his home (he lived with his wife and two daughters, even if this didn't in any way reduce his feelings of loneliness), but he felt a sacred respect for private property as well as for the integrity of a magazine in the waiting room of a dentist's office. He stuck it even lower, among the magazines that talked about movie stars, the love affairs of princesses and dukes, the latest technical advances in stereos and computers. He had the impulse to hide it behind the chair so that no one would find it, but he would have had to make a movement that others would have noticed. Everyone would dash to get the magazine, and on thumbing through the pages they would find the article by Mr. Irving Peele, psychologist at Anneversie Hospital in South Dakota.

He got rather nervous when one of the patients (the fellow who had entered last) stretched out his hand towards the glass table, removed the top two magazines that didn't interest him, and looked at the ones underneath with a certain hesitation until he decided upon one about motors with large illustrations in color.

As a precaution, he let the other waiting patients go before him, an act of unheard of courtesy. When the waiting room was finally empty, he breathed more calmly, now convinced that the secret was his more than ever before.

He walked with determination into the dentist's office and suddenly caught sight of the threatening drill still swinging from side to side like a furious bumble bee. He exchanged a few jokes with the dentist, who was happy to see him in such a good mood and less apprehensive than at other times. "The truth is, I have a secret," he told him smiling, and the dentist asked what it was. "I can't tell you," replied the patient. The dentist inserted the metal plate that was to keep his mouth open and began work with the drill, but he didn't go back to the topic of the secret. The man withstood the dentist's work without complaint and, when he was saying good-bye, made a comment about the soccer game the next Sunday.

He went out onto the street a new man, as if fixing his molar had also mended some other part of his personality. The streets were crowded, but this time the people didn't oppress him, didn't minimize him as they always used to do. "They have a secret, but they don't know it," he thought, looking at them with feelings of compassion and satisfaction at the same time. Better that Mr. Irving Peele hadn't appeared on television to publicize his discovery: this created a difference between himself and all the others.

He stopped in front of a store window featuring men's clothing with its group of elegant and well-dressed mannequins. He studied the beige jackets and shoes made of real leather.

"I have something that you don't have," he murmured in a soft voice.

Other times the suits and accessories had tempted him, making him feel inferior because he could never buy them. Now he looked at them without envy, as frivolous things of fleeting importance.

He strolled down the long avenue without haste, stopping here and there with great pleasure because now he was looking at things from another perspective. He lamented that the air was so polluted because otherwise he would have liked to have taken a deep breath. He saw the posters from an agency advertising trips, and he stopped in front of one with a reproduction of Hong Kong; that city seemed to him the most surprising and far-away place anyone could visit. He wasn't willing for Hong Kong to exist independently of any traveler: it was the type of place that only exists when someone goes there. Moreover, he couldn't be sure that the article by Mr. Irving Peele would apply in that far-off place.

He went into a bar and asked for a cognac. He did it naturally and freely, without the bad feeling that he used to have because he thought it was an excessive expense in a time of crisis. He was a man who had a secret, and the nature of the secret was such that it couldn't be revealed; he had to make do keeping it to himself.

A woman came over to him, and instead of becoming intimidated as usual (unsure of himself, his looks, his future, his past), he invited her to drink with him and offered her a cigarette.

The woman said he looked like an interesting man, and he answered that he had something that other men didn't have or didn't know they had. She laughed, thinking he was telling a somewhat obscene joke. He didn't seem to notice. But surprisingly, he became frightened; that woman, with her rather loose ways, couldn't she be trying to take away what he had, since he had been so imprudent as to reveal himself? To possess something—even if it were a secret—had turned him into a vain man who bragged about himself. He paid and left, regretting his frankness.

To have an identity and to know about it made him a more powerful person than others, but he shouldn't go around showing off his secret; it would cause suspicion and envy; someone might get the idea to steal it.

He thought of calling the girl from the park, the one he hadn't seen for a while because he didn't have anything to offer her. What could she expect from a mature man whom the crisis had left unemployed and who lacked the charm that could set him apart from other men? "Now I have something," he thought about telling her, but when he got to the phone booth he stopped because if she were to ask what the secret was he might not have the words to name it. If he had only pulled out the two pages from the magazine and kept them in his pocket, he could consult Dr. Peele; surely there was some reasonable explanation in the text but he didn't remember what it was.

He continued on his way, singing softly "I have a secret and nobody knows it." Finally he had something that no one could take away. Time had taken charge of getting rid of his youth while he fulfilled all the duties expected of a man: military service, marriage, work, daughters. The crisis took care of the rest: it took away his job, car, weekends in the mountains. Slowly he had been stripped of everything. ("Dust thou art and to dust thou shalt return," he recalled the biblical phrase), and now suddenly he had something again, but it was something of a secret nature, something he couldn't use to pay his debt at the bank or buy his daughters' clothes or his wife's false teeth, nor could it be exhibited like a hunting trophy but, nevetheless, it had a quality that nothing before had: according to Dr. Irving Peele it was something intransferable, something all his own that he could take with him even beyond the grave. He laughed. It was good to possess something, at last, even though it couldn't be detected (and perhaps precisely for this reason), it couldn't be lost.

On the way he met up with an ex-employee from work who had been dismissed at the same time as he. They weren't friends, but when they met a certain solidarity in misfortune led them to have a drink together. The loss of his job had embittered the fellow; he was more aggressive than before and he never smiled. They had two glasses of wine together, and he couldn't resist the temptation to tell him while the other had his head down looking at the wooden floor:

"I have a treasure."

The man lifted his head slowly, somewhat disbelievingly, and seemed to examine him carefully.

"Yes, it's true," he repeated with assurance. "I have a treasure."

Could he have won the lottery? Or perhaps he had a very valuable stamp? Someone had told the man that there were little pieces of paper that were worth a fortune; the problem lay in recognizing them. How would he know, for instance, when a stamp was worth something? Just like coins, but how were guys like them going to inherit a coin from the Roman Empire?

"It's not true," the man answered cautiously. "No one who has a fortune loses his job. If you had a treasure, you'd still be working because only those who don't have anything have things taken away from them."

"It's that my treasure is a secret," he said, asking for another glass of wine to show off a bit.

"A secret?" the fellow repeated, as if the words weighed on his lips. People with a lot of money had bank accounts in foreign countries. So nobody knew what they really had, not even members of their own families. This was a secret too. Could he have received some sort of inheritance? He threw out the idea immediately; only rich people received inheritances—poor people don't have anyone to inherit from. This was the way it was.

"I can't tell anyone," he added, as if apologizing but with some satisfaction.

The other man looked at him attentively, as if he could find the secret in his face. Afterwards he moved back a little, rested on the back of his chair and said with absolute certainty:

"They'll take it away from you."

This phrase made him shiver.

"Impossible," he answered.

"They'll take it away from you," insisted the other man. Haven't they already taken everything you had? The poor man only gets something so he can lose it," he proclaimed. "Didn't they take away your job? Didn't they take away your car? If now you have a treasure, they'll take that away too."

"They won't be able to," he said with assurance. "Not if I don't want them to. It's the only thing I have left."

He still had something to lose? The other man was amazed. "Whatever it is, take good care of it," he said in an act of spontaneous generosity.

"Yes, I'll take care of it," he answered and made a gesture to pay.

He found his wife watching television. It was an old set because they didn't have the money to get a new one, but it was on all day long. And still you could see something. For all that there was to see: police shows, old movies brought back year after year and some musicals that broke your eardrums. She said that it kept her company. Through the loneliness that attacked amidst the dirty dishes and lay in wait behind the furniture and neighbor's screams. Life had taken away everything: youth, job, weekends in the mountains, it had even taken away love. Could she too have a secret that she didn't know anything about? The article didn't say anything specific about women. Had Mr. Irving Peele forgotten all about them? Should one suppose that they were also included? Anyway, even if she were to possess a secret like his own, she didn't know it and that was the difference. "We aren't equal," he thought, and this satisfied him.

"Where were you?" asked his wife resentfully.

"Taking a walk," he responded briefly.

Life had also taken away the desire to make love along with all the other things.

"You seem to be happy," the woman murmured without taking her eyes off the television.

"I have a secret and no one knows about it," he thought secretly. Finally something that they couldn't steal from him. Something inalienable, the article had said, and he remembered the word because he didn't know exactly what it meant. Something that didn't fade away with time, something that they couldn't snatch away from him because of his age, or use against him like a document firing him or unpaid bills. Something wholly his own that, moreover, his daughters couldn't inherit. Only rich people leave inheritances, and his treasure was intransmissible.

"I have something nobody knows about and which is very valuable," he announced to his wife, because it seemed to him that having a treasure and not talking about it was like not having it at all.

She looked him up and down, incredulous.

"It's true," he affirmed. "I've just discovered it."

Her husband had never hit on the lottery, he hadn't even won any of the small local raffles. What was he up to now?

"Well, you should buy a suit," said the woman just in case. "And the water heater needs to be fixed."

He stopped short.

"It's not for those kinds of things," he responded after a bit.

She looked at him suspiciously.

"Just as I thought," she said. "So what is it good for then?"

He thought. The article had said that identity was inexpressible.

"I can't say," he answered.

"He's had too much to drink," she thought and went back to watching television.

He lay down in bed, in front of the open window that let in noises from throughout the building, and he looked at the whitewashed ceiling. Suddenly it seemed the secret wasn't that important. If he couldn't tell anyone about it, if it couldn't be used to buy a suit or have the water heater fixed, if it couldn't help him get back his desire to make love, what good was it? Surely only so they could take it away. And anybody could take it away, because he wasn't going to defend something he knew nothing about, something he couldn't even locate.

He didn't even have the pages from the magazine with the article by Mr. Peele. Maybe if he read it he could keep his secret, this treasure that now seemed to dissolve among the noise of dishes in the next apartment, the jumbled voices coming from the television set and the barking of a dog on the terrace above. It must be a vaporous secret that could evaporate like cigarette smoke. Had he smoked his treasure without knowing it when he came in tonight? Was it so fragile? And what if Dr. Peele had made a mistake? What if identity was something that only a few men had, like fortunes in Switzerland, land holdings, investments and sports cars? Maybe his ex-co-worker was right and that they'd already taken his treasure away along the road. Inadvertently, like he had lost everything else, but unavoidably, just as unavoidably as the other losses. Maybe he had only possessed the treasure for a few minutes, just long enough to have a drink with an unknown woman in a bar, to sing softly in front of a store window and to withstand the dentist's work.

He turned over in bed and tried to fall asleep. He heard water flowing from the tank and the monotonous cry of a child. His identity had also slipped away, like the water, and the sleep that was coming towards him was an anonymous sleep, shapeless, the sleep of someone who has no secrets.

A Useless Passion

I HAD ARRIVED in the city two days before, and I got lost easily. I have never been adept at plans and maps; in truth, for me they are unsettling hieroglyphics impossible to decipher, stones inscribed with a legend meant only for the initiated. I get lost in maps' grids—overlapping networks of red, blue and yellow lines, black dots and green numbers—a tiny insect in a haphazard forest.

When I got off the airplane, I felt a sort of hypnosis. I found myself in an enormous several storied airport which was really a city in miniature. Indicators overhead showed the way, like signals at a crosswalk. Illuminated signs guided the traveler like the stars that led the argonauts through the high seas. In the middle of the vast waxed surface of the airport, with my little suitcase in hand, I had a moment of indecision, of confusion. On my right was a big supermarket where passengers on international flights could buy bottles of whiskey, cognac, liquors and cigarettes at cheaper prices. On my left was a bookstore with revolving shelves full of books in English, detective and erotic novels, magazines on the economy, sports, movies, and crossword puzzles. At the entrance was a postcard stand where I went almost automatically. My horror of unknown cities is almost as great as my pleasure in bright shiny postcards depicting a garden full of yellow tulips, a fountain with flying Pegasuses and bearded gods, the white monkey—main attraction at the zoo—ancient artificially lighted churches, the Ferris wheel at the amusement park. With a pair of postcards like these in my pocket, I feel more secure, as if the city were built on a human scale and were really accessible.

There was a row of red plastic seats, like in a movie theater, in front of a video screen which showed unending panoramic images of beaches, casinos, parks, and islands. The airport also had a cafeteria—crammed full of passengers with leather attaché cases drinking cognac or soft drinks while talking eagerly about business—which I refused to enter on account of the noise, not to mention the enameled bathrooms, the shower rooms, the interminable line of ticket counters with their blue signs—Air India, Pan American, SAS, British Airlines, Avianca—and an extremely long moving passageway which transported motionless travelers like a collection of mannequins.

I could have bought stamps, boxes of chocolates, cameras, handkerchiefs, porcelain plates with pictures of typical landscapes painted on them, leather belts, matches, bottles of perfume, liquors, English biscuits, deodorants and stuffed animals. I could have stayed in the airport forever and life wouldn't have changed a bit. I thought of a great green and transparent aquarium whose fish hung motionless, swimming in an unchanging environment of stones and seaweed.

An illuminated moving sign near the ceiling showed the temperature in Moscow (9 degrees), Cairo (14), Copenhagen (7), Tokyo (12), Zurich (4), Bonn (6), and Rio de Janeiro (16). A group of electronic clocks announced the time in Madrid, Mexico and New York. And in each of these cities, world travelers (how precise the word becomes in this case!) were waiting next to a counter, closing business deals, and drinking whiskey while the airplanes (Barcelona–Chicago, London–Amsterdam, Buenos Aires–Santiago, Helsinki–Los Angeles), like giant bees, were resting on the runways and taking on fuel.

I felt like calling my wife. Little plastic telephone booths, all the same like the hair dryers in beauty shops, were lined up in front of me. With their heads submerged inside, anonymous travelers were doing their best to have conversations through lines that imperceptibly crossed the ocean. But I stopped myself; my wife was on another continent, at another time and in another season of the year, and both realities, while simultaneous, couldn't be taken in at the same time; the effectiveness of any act depends on the absurd belief that there is only one reality. Mine for the moment was centered upon this airport that I should try to leave to take a taxi to the hotel, breaking the spell of this fish tank with its bright surfaces.

What is strange is hostile. When I got to the hotel I found out that the man I was to see and who was mainly responsible for my trip had died a few hours earlier of a sudden heart attack.

The news upset me. My difficulties with a new language made me doubt the information; I thought I had misunderstood and I kept asking, repeating the name of my host.

"He's dead," confirmed the unknown voice at the other end of the phone.

"Dead?" I repeated before hanging up in an almost automatic way.

When I travel I have the feeling that the act of moving in time and space breaks a mysterious geometry of things carefully intertwined, and that this rupture will have unknown and unexpected consequences which get reproduced and multiply, thereby transforming the order of the universe. Mr. G., manager of a publishing house that was going to put out a little book of poems I had written some time before in my language and in my city, had died unexpectedly in the exact moment in which I was traveling to see him.

I stayed in the hotel lobby, unsettled. My head, as if separated from the rest of my body, was making endless attempts to reconstruct the past to make the numbers of my life somehow coincide with those of Mr. G., in two different cities separated by thousands of kilometers, one of which was in an autumn full of mist and the other a springtime of white almond blossoms. In effect, I had traveled ten hours in a plane, in spite of which I arrived at G.'s city only four hours after my departure. There was, then, six hours of difference, and in these six hours which I was supposed to live twice, G. had died in his city, but he did not die for me who had six hours advantage over him. If G. had died—as they told me—five hours before my arrival, I still had an hour to find him, to try the impossible, to find G. He was probably waiting for me somewhere in the city anxious to make our appointment, to make our times coincide and then to say good-bye in a period of time that would let him die also for me.

The six hours which separated me from the people in G.'s city turned me into an old man, a man who has the rare opportunity to live a piece of his life twice, knowing moreover in advance some of the things that were going to happen in the next few hours. But this knowledge turned me into a solitary being as well, a man who was going to live six hours of his life twice but who couldn't share this repetition with anyone. I thought of those stars at an enormous distance, gigantic reservoirs of the past in which our modern astrophysicists contemplate the simultaneity of all things (Homer and Shakespeare, Hitler and Napoleon, the wheel and the telephone, the silex knife and laser beam, dinosaurs and Buster Keaton). The stars' memory stops exactly a moment before the original big bang *because they still aren't old enough to remember it.* Perhaps only G. in some part of this inhospitable city knew beforehand, as did I, what was going to happen and, once dead to his fellow citizens, was using up the period that separated us to die, this time definitively in the time that I had left. So I had to hurry if I wanted to find him still alive and say good-bye. One doesn't travel to meet a dead man, but rather a live one. But, how do we find someone who in spite of being about to die is a stranger, someone whose face, age, favorite spots, customs, little habits and whims we don't know? How to find him in a city where we aren't familiar with the parks, bridges, avenues or plazas?

I went out. An anonymous traveler floating between tall buildings made of steel and glass whose beauty, if indeed they had any, was foreign to me; among complicated roadways whose end points I did not know; words and phrases which demanded my entire attention if I wanted to figure out what they said; work and routines begun when I was not yet there and which would continue on when I left, the useless passion of the traveler.

I decided to call my wife; I needed support, like a small child lost in an enormous metal construction, a familiar reference point in a world that was alien and strange to me. I went off to a public phone, dialed the number and waited. It seemed to me that the signal was different, but surely the distance (that enormous distance that separated me in time and space) made the tone change.

No one answered. A quick calculation made me think that my wife was possibly out of the house, innocently doing the day's shopping, not knowing that G. was about to die and that I, a stranger in the city, was obliged to find him while I walked with no specific direction and looked around bewildered at stores whose names I didn't know, the artificial fountains, the bookstores full of books in another language.

In the hotel they had not been able to give me any information about Mr. G. or the company he worked for. I hastened to tell them that it was a business matter and, solicitous, they handed me a map of the city with the principal monuments, three-star restaurants, casinos, night spots and rental car agencies all marked. I thought of Mr. G. as, in a fog, I walked down unknown streets. I didn't know if he were young or old, if he lived in the country or in the city. He had written me a letter some time before expressing a certain interest in a small volume of poems I had written. The letter, typed with the name and address of the publishing company, didn't have any more information. There were just a few lines, very correct and courteous to be sure, but brief; perhaps Mr. G. had difficulty writing in a language not his own, or he was a very busy man who avoided trifles. The second time he wrote to me was to arrange the date of my trip, and he added this or that polite detail, reminding me, for instance, of the change of seasons in this hemisphere and the importance of reserving a room in a small comfortable hotel in this city plagued by tourists.

I thought about it while I ambled through G.'s city, a foreigner who had to repeat six hours of his time in order to live simultaneously with the men and women of this city, a foreigner who already knew what was going to happen in an hour (because this hour had already been lived up there in the airplane), in spite of which I could do nothing to prevent it. And I had to relive this time lapse in a city which wasn't mine, under an unfamiliar sky, whose light seemed odd to me. It was that unstable hour in which the night has not yet begun but the day has already ended; the imprecise colors render the shapes of things and faces almost unreal, and one's spirit plunges into a dread of the void. As if everybody at this moment felt the same horror at the void, I noticed that the passers-by went scurrying down to the metro stations or to bus stops without looking right or left, fearful perhaps at what was left behind or what was coming at them if they didn't flee immediately.

I tried to imagine where Mr. G. would take refuge every afternoon at the end of work, when the sky changed its light and the shape of things dissolved. Was there a café that Mr. G. went to in order to pass the time as night came in with its own rhythm, making it easier then to withstand his feelings of termination? Or a club with its green carpets, the clock on the wall, familiar faces and the solicitous waiter who already knows what cocktail to serve? Did Mr. G. go visit a lady in the sad hours of the afternoon in order to drown between the sheets and comfortable maternal breasts the painful sensation of the death of everything?

If G. had died five hours before my arrival, I had very little time left to find him alive and, even while I was a confused and surprised foreigner—like all foreigners—I had to hurry to make our appointment. The six hours of difference that separated me from the rest of the people in this city gave me a rare privilege: G. was not dead for me, and only for me, and my obligation was to find him.

I gave the driver the address of the publishing company, and I let him drive me there without putting up any resistance, relieved to surrender to someone. The taxi dropped me in front of a large red glass and metal building of a modern style. The doors and windows, in strange geometric shapes, were closed and covered with iron sheets like a gigantic suit of armor on a medieval knight. Surely this was a residential neighborhood because I didn't see anyone on the streets. All had already fled the afternoon and were probably taking refuge in their houses or inside the bars. I didn't find a single sign to tell me that there was a publishing company in this enormous building protected like a warrior, but then again I didn't know the customs of the city, and it could have been placed somewhere else or behind the metal curtain.

I looked for Mr. G. in the surrounding areas. I had the crazy hope that he was waiting there, aware of the urgency of our meeting and my difficulty in finding him in any other way. But the street was empty and the outskirts too. There was no one between the trees or inside the parked cars, abandoned quickly by their drivers as soon as they had locked up, as if they were fearful of staying out in the approaching darkness.

One of the few passers-by still out in the streets came up to me, all stirred up, and babbled some words I didn't manage to understand. I offered him a light, a cigarette, but he didn't seem to need either and quickly went away, leaving me alone. I thought he possibly had wanted to warn me about something; I wasn't familiar with the customs of the city, and it could have been that there was an alarm, a fire or an air raid test. There was no bar nearby where G. could have been waiting for me, and when I looked at my watch I realized that I had only a few minutes left to find him; he would die after these minutes were up, and I would have made the trip in vain. The streets seemed all the same to me. Unlike the common observer, I can only appreciate things as a whole—details escape me; for this reason it's difficult for me to distinguish between two like things. I decided to call my wife again. I needed to hear a familiar voice. I went to a telephone booth in the street and dialed. I waited anxiously for the signal. The phone was busy. I didn't hang up, hoping that the conversation would be a short one. But surely the ocean, the change of time and hemisphere had interfered with our telepathy; when I dialed again, the phone was still busy. I couldn't lose more time and so I hung up, uneasy.

I thought that somewhere in this now deserted city, surely this very second, G. would be looking for me, hurrying rapidly through his last moments, anxious to find me and to make this unpostponable appointment. I supposed that G. would have naturally gone to the hotel and, satisfied with this new hope, I got in a taxi. It seemed to me that the return ride wasn't the same, but I couldn't trust my impressions; I don't have a sense of direction and places don't seem familiar if the direction I'm going is not the same. Since the night had already fallen, I noticed that there were people in the streets, in front of shop windows and restaurants. Could G. have been among the passers-by, unaware of his fate, frivolously using up what was his last hour for me? If it were so, I couldn't recognize him among the crowds, and our meeting would never take place.

G. wasn't in the hotel. I asked the concierge about him, without any luck. He hadn't left a message for me either. My wife hadn't called me, as I supposed, nor had G. There were only a few minutes left before the hour was up, and I felt completely discouraged. I called the publishing company again, in case some employee staying late could provide some information, but the metallic voice of an answering machine informed me that the company was closed until Monday. It was Friday night. Suddenly I realized that if G. died without my having found him, I'd be completely alone in the city; nobody, absolutely nobody knew me; I'd be the only witness to my trip, and this might never have taken place.

I decided to wait sitting on one of the hotel sofas. I tried to thumb through a newspaper, but I was tired and the letters, combined in different ways than those in my native language, didn't give me much information. I lit a cigarette but I became afraid of dying and I put it out. Any movement that I made, no matter how small, uncovered that watch on my wrist and its implacable hands closing in on the exact moment in which G. was going to die, also for me. Definitively dead. There were only a scarce five minutes left when the hotel's revolving door turned on its axis and a tall man, impeccably dressed in gray, appeared and went over to the reception desk. He was blond with blue eyes that seemed exceptionally bright. He didn't look to be more than forty-five. With my heart beating wildly, I got up and went over to greet him. I extended a sweaty hand; I hadn't eaten or slept in many hours, the expectation had exhausted all my nerves and I needed, among other things, a good bath. But I thought that none of these things had much importance if G. were still alive and could shake my hand.

Somewhat embarrassed by my attitude, the man greeted me courteously and as soon as he noticed my accent, introduced himself in his own language. He wasn't G., didn't know him, and had never heard anything about him. He was staying at the hotel, like me, and was asking for his key at the desk.

I looked at my watch. At this exact moment G. had just died. Slowly I went up to a telephone booth. Incapable of dialing myself, I asked for an assisted call and gave my home phone number and my wife's name. I waited for a short time, leaning against the side of the booth where somebody had carved a name and a date. Somebody had been there a year before who possibly hadn't met anybody and who carved his name and date with a sharp instrument in order to leave some proof of his presence, just like prisoners do.

The operator's cold and distant voice on the other end of the line said:

"Wrong name and number."

I paled. I was very tired and moreover G. had died, but I didn't think I had made a mistake, perhaps it was the operator who had misunderstood, what with the ocean, the night, the long trip, the change of seasons, the unknown streets, the different language. I persisted. I asked her to call again and, so I didn't make a mistake, I wrote down all the information on a piece of paper which I read slowly, repeating the numbers and letters. I waited. I listened to the telephone ring in another country, at another hour of the day, in autumn not in spring.

The operator's voice—far away as if submerged in time—informed me:

"Wrong name and number."

The Mirror Maker

HE MAKES MIRRORS. And he is a solitary man who lives in the mirrors' houses and mute faces. Often when you look for him, you find a mirror in his place, so tightly anchored to the floor that it is impossible to move. The visitor then speaks to the mirror as if its builder were nearby, or leaves a message on the frame with no doubt that it will be seen.

He builds mirrors of all sizes, from little ones that you carry in a pocket to great Venetian mirrors that decorate palace salons and the walls of illustrious homes. He also builds them in several shapes: there are oval mirrors and mirrors that are triangular or round; there are mirrors in the shape of a wave, a window, the sun and one time he even built a mirror in the shape of a human face which so bothered people who looked at themselves in it that he decided—he is a careful man—to take it off the wall where he had placed it. He is the creator of several mirrors in the shape of columns that decorate an atrium (of a summer palace) and of a mirror in the shape of a lake that confuses many people, where royal swans swim about but so far away that you can't tell if they are nude or wearing clothes.

It's said that there are no desires he can't satisfy. He built a pink mirror for a melancholy man, one that multiplied gold coins for a very greedy one, another that reflected only landscapes for a misogynous philosopher, and they say he built the strangest mirror in the world, one in which figures slide like liquids and through which bodies cross rapidly, leaving a delicate blue halo from their passing. Someone said that this was really a mirror of souls, not of bodies, and that the fleeting trace on the mercury was the ghost of spirits that cannot see one another, but he refused to confirm or deny this statement.

Inside his house (silently closed up and to which no one has access) he safeguards those unique mirrors he will never be able to build again and he will never sell to anybody: the mirror like a slow watch that only reflects the day before, the mirror of our dreams (which he usually keeps covered with a blanket and uncovers only a few times each year, just often enough to keep himself from dying), the mirror of memory (he only lets children look in it), the sleepwalking mirror (we see its images even when we're asleep) and the mirror of love, which superimposes two figures, trait by trait, into one single face, one single body (a chilling vision that few have been able to tolerate.)

Now he is working on his most ambitious project: to build a wall of mercury that will surround the city. He is planning to erect a huge mirror that will act as a border and will stand like a wall, reproducing in great detail the insides of every house: the human beings who live there, the animals, trees, towers, temples, brothels, birds, statues, theaters, shops, military men, schools, plazas and stadiums. Upon looking out the window, each person will be able to contemplate, as if he or she were in a theater, an enormous spectacle of multiplicity and fragmentation. The mirror maker thinks that in this way the many errors of thought and behavior attributable to a lack of awareness about the infinite simultaneity of the real will tend to be fewer, and the person who, out of cowardice or laziness, still maintains that he is the center of the world will have a daily confrontation with the mirror that never sleeps. He adds, moreover, that many people will want to correct the errors in the mirror and that this will ennoble the life of the city.

Since he is not absolutely sure of being understood by his contemporaries (just like other artists), the mirror maker has planned to retire to the outskirts of the city as soon as his immense wall of mercury has been completed. Moreover he is sure of dying when the very last section is finally built, and then, meticulously, the inhabitants of the city can confirm the incessant spectacle of multiplicity and fragmentation.

The Bell Ringer

THAT NO ONE LIVES IN THE VILLAGE isn't reason enough for him to stop ringing the bell every day. That the church door is closed doesn't deter him, not even when he has to get to the bell tower by climbing through a wooden window whose slats are falling apart and creak with the wind. Luckily the hinges have snapped, and it takes little effort to go through the window; nevertheless, the very long stairway, twisting and full of turns, presents numerous obstacles he can't always avoid without harm. The steps are worn away by dampness and rust, no light brightens his ascent, and sometimes he has to frighten away the bats that fly in his face; rats have eaten the lime from the once whitewashed walls and columns, so it's not good to lean on them; cockroaches, who overrun the staircase, climb up his ankles and spiders jump from the ceiling like parachutists. When he slips and falls, he grabs onto a rotten piece of wood, curses the abandonment of the place and that there is no kind of protection—either official or private—for the bell tower. Even he himself is too lazy to spend time fixing the staircase or his impatience won't permit it; his only objective is to ring the bell, not reconstruct the church.

When he gets to the bell tower, exhausted, he looks around. From up high he contemplates a flat expanse of land which has not been tilled, a vast countryside of many colors, mute and mild under the dawn lights (he goes up early because he believes that the bell shouldn't be put off, even if there is no one around). Some three hundred houses of pink and blue stone, with pathetic and weak weeds sprouting out of their sides, stand up against a grayish sky cut through by lilac clouds.

The stones join together like a small fortress in the desert. The sky seems immense, the land very open. Not a sound is heard except for the wind, whose blowing is more intense up there in the bell tower. It is a stony landscape, without water in spite of the dark clouds and the sound of leaves rustling in the distance. He thinks of it as a strange uninhabited manger; on the endless plains there are only houses made of stone and pathways going down made of rock. There are no animals, no people, no birds in the entire landscape that his eyes can take in from the bell tower. Not a single sheep. Not a river. If there is a rumble of thunder, it seems to come from another sky.

The houses in this abandoned village have their doors shut tight, just like the church. But this has not kept the passing or looting stranger from going through the windows and taking the few things of value that were left behind: coffee grinders with handles, grinding wheels, hand plows. As when someone took off with the gold chalice and purple altar cloth.

In this quiet and stony landscape, he stands up for an instant, looking out at the immensity of the gray sky, the size of this uncultivated land where only thistles and shrubs are growing. The weeds move and the stable door creaks, neighing at the wind like a rebellious colt. Then he suddenly makes the bell ring. The loud clangings are exact and solemn; he is a competent worker, a responsible man. He rings the bell with expertise and with just the right emphasis at just the right time. The clapper swings heavily as he makes regular genuflections while holding on to the cord. The bell's swinging takes him from an extreme of dark and green countryside covered with bushes to the other extreme of the land, clearer now, where the last houses make their stand. He knows that the village is empty in the flat barrenness of this denuded land, but he suspects, and sometimes even holds the conviction, that the bell rings in another sky.

The Sentence

THE PICTURE BY IVAN BULGAKOV, a Russian painter unknown to me, was of a completely black sea that blended (one
couldn't figure out how) into an enormous sky of the same color.
Without a horizontal line, the uniform blackness filled the canvas. Nevertheless, the depth of the brushwork revealed that the
sea and the sky were not at all alike. There were hidden whirl-
winds, forces in motion that had not yet come to the surface. In
the black vastness (the painter seemed to be concerned with
expressing a sense of infinity) there was a little gray figure. It was
a war ship, lost between the sky and the sea, whose dangerous
mission I did not know. It was so small, almost in the center of
the canvas, that I had the sensation that night had taken over the
museum walls, bringing them into the painting with a certain
majesty. I went closer to separate the walls from the rest of the
canvas and it was then that I noticed a light in the gray unifor-
mity of the little boat. It was true, the painter had lit up the
boat's railing with a yellow light, like a light bulb. And there was
someone hanging in the center of this circle. I didn't figure out
if it was a man or a woman; the figure, so very far into the distance, had been drawn with very few strokes as if it were a warn-
ing instead of a person. I ran away from this ghostly vision like
an escaping prisoner.

I tried to contain my excitement, and I went off quickly to
another hallway where more benign paintings were on exhibit.
Flower pots, girls with hats on Mediterranean beaches, Gauguin's
light. But my eyes wandered over the different canvasses as if

they were slipping, incapable of stopping before the stain of color of a dress or the vague smoke from a train. I had been in Lake Como, painted by Xavier Valls in 1973, and had seen the fluid vapor that rises up the mountain, but the other image, the one of the black sea with its gray war ship and hanging figure, seemed much more real to me than the transparencies of a Vermont forest painted by Adrian Lawrence in 1979, the same year that I had been there.

The painting by Ivan Bulgakov didn't have a date, and I searched in vain for one among the tiny letters of the catalogue. This vaguely unnerved me. I would have liked to anchor the painting to something, even if it were only the numbers of a date. Maybe it was this uncertainty that pushed me towards it once again. Anxiety made me go through the hallway again as if I had lost something. For some strange reason, nobody was looking at it. The visitors were going over to other bigger paintings, less anguished ones. I stopped and stared at the little gray boat. Again I saw the yellow light that reminded me of a bare bulb and the outline of a hanging figure in the middle of an intense darkness. If I took my eyes away, I was lost in the black immensity of the sea, or was it of the sky ? The brilliant brush strokes almost came together. I remained a few minutes under its spell until the intensity of the blackness frightened me, and I turned to flee again.

At the museum's exit there was a counter with reproductions. I looked eagerly through the illustrations and postcards for the painting by Bulgakov. It wasn't there. This disappointed me. I wanted to leave, but I wanted somehow to hold on to my memory of the painting. But no, I already had the memory. What I wanted was to have a small reproduction in my pocket that I could take out at any time, get used to looking at it until, having seen it so many times, it stopped being so painful. Until

I could discover its mystery. If there was one. Because it's also possible that the painting was done many centuries ago by an enlightened painter who put on canvas an image that we all have inside us. It was possible, too, that I had painted this picture in one of my nightmares and the trembling it gave me was one of recognition. Perhaps the painting was from my past, inscribed in some unknown convolution of my brain, and Bulgakov had found it out.

Without the reproduction I couldn't get myself to abandon the museum or to leave the painting alone on the wall, although it is also possible that the one who didn't want to remain alone was me. To be close to the painting excited me too much; to be away from it plunged me into helplessness. There was a cafeteria in the museum lobby which seemed to be a good middle ground which could protect me from making any decision; it was neither close to nor far away from the painting. I could leave or return. I went over there.

It was a room with white walls and blue tables and chairs. Visitors to the museum, tired from walking around, rested there with their bags gaping open and legs hanging limp. There were Germans, French and Belgians. There were different languages. I don't know why, but this soothed me.

The museum cafeteria seemed like a place outside of space and time; that is, somewhere away from any kind of anguish. It suddenly occurred to me that no painter I knew of had painted this exact scene: a museum cafeteria like a railway platform for tired travelers who have just arrived at a station where time and space no longer count. But if Bulgakov had painted a dark nightmare that I or someone else had dreamt hundreds of years before, so too it was possible that somewhere in the world— today or tomorrow—in Amsterdam, San Francisco, Tripoli or Buenos Aires, someone was going to be painting the scene.

Therefore the painting I was imagining already existed. Like Bulgakov's, it had lived in my unconscious all along.

There was a window, and through it I saw a narrow path lined with poplar trees. The scene comforted me, and I was able to look around with ease. At one table there was an older married couple, surely North American, whose appearance remained youthful in spite of their ages. Four or five Japanese students were talking not far from the window. Two slightly affected men were having coffee at another table. I looked across the room at a diagonal, and against the background of a white wall I discovered a blond girl dressed in blue. She was alone, and from her appearance I couldn't figure out her nationality. She was drinking a glass of something dark that seemed to be wine, and I was surprised that they would serve wine in a museum. Her features were so delicate they seemed washed out, as if they had gotten lost in her hair. This made me curious. I approached her. She didn't seem too disturbed by my presence; perhaps she was merely indifferent. I have a good ear and when she said two words I recognized her accent. I speak three languages; I knew hers well. Right away I realized that her conversation was as evasive as her features: her eyebrows dissolved into her brow which disappeared behind her blond hair, her delicate lips got lost in the whiteness of her cheeks, her ears fled toward the nape of her neck just like her conversation, which was made up of little interjections whose meaning remained ambiguous. She *was* drinking wine in fact, and I invited her to have another. I told her that she looked vaguely familiar, which was not an attempt at seduction but rather a feeling I had. I thought I had seen her face somewhere, in a city, on a lake, mountain, railway platform or boat. She put me off: she traveled very little; really she only took a few short trips to this city that wasn't her own and that she didn't know very well, and that she didn't have much interest in getting to know better. She didn't need a guide, then: she liked to be alone and to think that she had great spaces of time before her to learn the names of streets, plazas, parks, churches and museums.

"Do you know that only foreigners visit museums in cities?" I asked her. She smiled.

"I am a foreigner," she said, briefly.

Of course she was, even though her appearance did not betray her; it was her accent that drew attention to her, making her different. But I was convinced that I had seen her face—not her accent—somewhere before.

I asked her how much time she could let pass before she had to learn the city, to wander over it little by little in an act that didn't have the languor of love, but rather the boredom. She answered vaguely. She didn't seem to suffer from that most common illness: believing that we are really the masters of time. Her sense of time seemed abstract, that of those condemned to purgatory.

"Can you leave or stay as you please?" I asked out of curiosity.

"Something like that," she answered without giving more details.

Bulgakov's painting also lacked a date.

I spoke to her about the city's museum of anthropology, which held some valuable pieces. She didn't seem too interested. Nor in the aquarium. It was a little better with the Great Conservatory: she had some fondness for music. Without realizing it, I was getting excited about my role as guide, and I also spoke to her about the wooden balustrade overlooking the sea from which to watch the slow movements of the ships going out to the bay, about the walkway with its slanted columns, and the rock in the shape of a horse.

"If you are so familiar with the city, you too must be a foreigner," she teased.

"My parents were," I answered quickly.

I had seen that face somewhere else. But she withstood my probing, like a hard rock. Like a ship's railing constantly whipped by the sea.

Although she tried to answer my questions with evasions, I had the sensation that they didn't bother her and that my presence was in some way pleasant for her. I know the loneliness of the foreigner; my parents had lived it. I know how one appreciates a smile, a friendly manner. Now I was the native and she the foreigner. This put me in a privileged position: that of being able to give without receiving in return.

"What's your occupation?" I asked abruptly. Right away I realized that this was a rather anachronistic way of asking what she did. I wanted to know if she had studied, if she had a profession, how she earned a living. She didn't seem surprised by my old-fashioned question, and I deduced that others had asked her the same many times before.

"I weave," she responded tiredly.

I imagined her hands—which were beautiful—elegantly grasping the shuttle.

I laughed. It was an occupation that I had forgotten about but perhaps one that was appropriate to confess in a museum.

"You don't look like one of Rembrandt's spinners," I said too brusquely. Her expression turned somewhat severe.

"And you in principle don't look like a policeman," she responded violently.

I felt hurt. Bulgakov's aggressive painting came to mind. The yellow light on the railing with its hanging figure. A punishment? A terrible revenge? And the darkness of the sky and sea, complete.

I didn't remember having used the word *police* more than twice in my life; it was so alien to me that on hearing it on her lips I felt a shudder of horror. She must have noticed, because after a while she added:

"Forgive me. It would be too much to explain. Questioning brings bad memories."

Suddenly I caught a glimpse of the geography of a country—hers—and some long ago news in the papers. I remembered too my parents' country and the apparent silence about a war.

"Do you like the museum?" I asked to relieve the tension.

"Yes," she answered. The calm. The absence of time. Space crystallized.

It was the same in Bulgakov's painting but nevertheless one was aware of a dark foreboding.

"I come here frequently to rest," she added, suddenly generous in her explanations. "I almost never look at the paintings or, at most, I pick out a vase of flowers to copy on the loom. I'm not an artist. I feel comfortable in the museum, as if I were away from any pressure. I work in a studio with other women, all from my country. Some weave birds and trees, plants and animals that don't exist here, that live in our memory. But I prefer to forget. I come to the museum and copy a still life, some flowers, an English landscape from the last century."

"Did you ever meet up with a painting that you knew, without ever having seen it before?" I asked while hiding my uneasiness.

She looked at me with some surprise.

"Listen," she said. "I don't know what idea you have of me. I'm from the country, not the city. I had never been in a museum before. I didn't know Van Gogh's name. Well maybe so, but I had never seen one of his paintings."

"It's not important," I said. "I'm asking if you have ever been in front of a painting that you've never seen before and felt as if you knew it well, as if perhaps you had painted it yourself."

"This only happens to me with people," she clarified.

"Suddenly when I am walking down a street in this city that I barely know, I think I recognize someone. I get excited, I start to shake. Nevertheless I know it is not possible; the person can't be here, the person has probably died or disappeared. But I think I see him or her. Then I start to cry."

I also felt moved. I couldn't specify the nature of the emotion nor its exact origin, but I felt the dampness of my hands and a certain palpitation in my abdomen. Now I was sure that I hadn't seen her in any street, nor on a platform, nor at the movies, nor at a theater's exit. Those indistinct features dissolved into her hair, the paleness of her face, the fearful air about her I had seen somewhere else. They were inside me, with all the certainty of a symbol.

"There's a Russian painter," I informed her, "named Ivan Bulgakov. Do you know him?"

It seemed that she was not indifferent to the name and that she was making an effort to remember.

"Excuse me," she replied. "My memory has been somewhat imprecise ever since I came to this city. I think it's a defense mechanism; I need to forget many unpleasant things and perhaps with them I also forget others that were pleasurable. It's possible that memory may be selective, but forgetting certainly is not. Nevertheless, Bulgakov, I seem to remember the name but I couldn't tell you exactly from where. There were many people of Russian descent in my country. Perhaps one of them..."

"Painter," I said trying to be precise.

"The professions..." she murmured and didn't continue the sentence.

"I'd like you to accompany me to one of the galleries," I invited. "Only for a moment. You won't get tired. I promise you that the visit will be brief."

Just then I realized that she had taken off her shoes under the table, and now she was looking for her sandals with her toes without bothering to look down.

I took her through a passageway to our left. I was so excited that I couldn't speak. She seemed to have entered into one of those raptures of lassitude in which not only her features but her entire face dissolved: a passenger from another space was getting lost in time.

We avoided an overladen still life, a fresh nude by Bonnard, the radiant light of a seashore by Sorolla, the majesty of a portrait from the eighteenth century. I went directly to the Bulgakov. There it was, all alone, enclosing the wall's brightness within its dark night. Black, intense, forsaken, nightmarish.

I took her arm with determination and placed her directly in front of the painting with all the severity of a revelation. In the middle of the dark canvas, in the middle of the sea as black as the insides of a whale and of the sky sprayed with pitch was a little war ship, gray. Above the barely drawn railing was a circle of yellow light. And hanging, subjected to the winds and tides, lost in the blackness without time or space, a hanging figure. A blond figure, without a face, with dissolving features, tied there like a punishment.

In front of the painting she let loose a horrible scream and put her hand to her mouth.

"Ivan Bulgakov," I murmured, from the deepest part of my being. 1816, 1850, 1895, 1914, 1917, 1939, 1941, 1953, 1968, 1973, 1975...: 'The Sentence.'

Singing in the Desert

THE FACT THAT SHE SINGS in the desert shouldn't surprise anybody since many people have done so since the beginning of time, when everything was sand (and also sky) and the oceans were frozen over.

We know that they sang in the desert, but we didn't listen to them, so we could say that up to a certain point they sang for themselves, although, in principle, this was not the purpose of their song.

Since we didn't hear them, we could also doubt that they ever sang at all; nevertheless we are sure that their voices rise or rose above the desert sands with the same kind of certainty that allows us to affirm that the earth is round without our having seen its shape, or that it rotates around the sun without our having any proof that we are moving. It's this kind of conviction that makes us suppose that they have sung in the desert even though we haven't heard them. Because song is one of the things that people do, and deserts really do exist.

She sings in a low voice. The sands are white and the sky yellow. She is sitting on a small dune with her eyes closed, and the dust covers her neck, eyelashes, and lips, from which a wisp of voice escapes like a sweet liquor onto the parched land. She sings without anyone listening, in spite of which we are certain that she is singing or that she has sung at one time.

Surely the wisp of her voice gets lost almost immediately in the motionless yellow space that surrounds her. And the sun, voraciously sucking the few drops of water up from a nearby lake, furiously drinks up the notes of her song. She doesn't stop singing nor does she sing louder; she keeps singing in the middle of the white sands and the pyramids of salt that arise like temples to a blind and dull-witted god. The sands, that have devoured more than one camel and its rider, hide the notes of her song. But the next day (or the next night, because although we can't hear it we can imagine that she also sings under the dark sky in the solitude of the desert), she lifts up her voice once more. Such persistence shouldn't surprise anybody for it seems somewhat intrinsic to song and sometimes intrinsic to the desert. So much so that it would be difficult for us to imagine a desert without a woman stationed on a sand dune, singing without being listened to.

We don't know the nature of the song although we are convinced that the song exists. When she comes down to the city (because she's not always in the desert; sometimes she participates in our city life and performs the conventional acts that we have been repeating ever since we were born), we accept her like just another inhabitant because, in truth, nothing distinguishes her from the rest of us except the fact that she sings in the desert, and we can forget this since nobody hears her. When she disappears again, we suppose that she has returned to the desert and that in the middle of the white sands and the sky like an ocean, she lifts up her voice, elevating her song that, like a drop of water dropped from space, is swallowed up by the dune.

ABOUT THE TRANSLATOR

Mary Jane Treacy is a professor of Spanish at Simmons College in Boston. Her interest in the work of Cristina Peri Rossi follows her interest in contemporary Latin American women's fiction, U.S. Latina literature, and women and violence in Latin American literature. Treacy previously translated Peri Rossi's fiction for publication in *Secret Weavers: Stories of the Fantastic by Women of Argentina and Chile*, ed. by Marjorie Agosin (White Pine Press, 1992).

ABOUT THE AUTHOR

Cristina Peri Rossi was born in Montevideo in Uruguay in 1941. In 1972 she went into exile in Spain where she writes for *Diario 16*, *El Periodico*, and *Agencia Efe*. Her many books of fiction, essays and poetry have been published in Spanish, English, German, Dutch, Italian, Portuguese, French, Hebrew, Swedish and Polish.

Books from Cleis Press

FICTION

Another Love
by Erzsébet Galgóczi.
ISBN: 0-939416-52-2 24.95 cloth;
ISBN: 0-939416-51-4 8.95 paper.

*Cosmopolis: Urban Stories by
Women* edited by Ines Rieder.
ISBN: 0-939416-36-0 24.95 cloth;
ISBN: 0-939416-37-9 9.95 paper.

A Forbidden Passion
by Cristina Peri Rossi.
ISBN: 0-939416-64-0 24.95 cloth;
ISBN: 0-939416-68-9 9.95 paper.

In the Garden of Dead Cars
by Sybil Claiborne.
ISBN: 0-939416-65-4 24.95 cloth;
ISBN: 0-939416-66-2 9.95 paper.

Night Train To Mother
by Ronit Lentin.
ISBN: 0-939416-29-8 24.95 cloth;
ISBN: 0-939416-28-X 9.95 paper.

*The One You Call Sister:
New Women's Fiction*
edited by Paula Martinac.
ISBN: 0-939416-30-1 24.95 cloth;
ISBN: 0-939416031-X 9.95 paper.

Only Lawyers Dancing
by Jan McKemmish.
ISBN: 0-939416-70-0 24.95 cloth;
ISBN: 0-939416-69-7 9.95 paper.

*Unholy Alliances: New Women's
Fiction* edited by Louise Rafkin.
ISBN: 0-939416-14-X 21.95 cloth;
ISBN: 0-939416-15-8 9.95 paper.

The Wall by Marlen Haushofer.
ISBN: 0-939416-53-0 24.95 cloth;
ISBN: 0-939416-54-9 paper.

LATIN AMERICA

*Beyond the Border: A New Age in
Latin American Women's Fiction*
edited by Nora Erro-Peralta and
Caridad Silva-Núñez.
ISBN: 0-939416-42-5 24.95 cloth;
ISBN: 0-939416-43-3 12.95 paper.

*The Little School: Tales of
Disappearance and Survival in
Argentina* by Alicia Partnoy.
ISBN: 0-939416-08-5 21.95 cloth;
ISBN: 0-939416-07-7 9.95 paper.

Revenge of the Apple
by Alicia Partnoy.
ISBN: 0-939416-62-X 24.95 cloth;
ISBN: 0-939416-63-8 8.95 paper.

You Can't Drown the Fire: Latin American Women Writing in Exile edited by Alicia Partnoy. ISBN: 0-939416-16-6 24.95 cloth; ISBN: 0-939416-17-4 9.95 paper.

AUTOBIOGRAPHY, BIOGRAPHY, LETTERS

Peggy Deery: An Irish Family at War by Nell McCafferty. ISBN: 0-939416-38-7 24.95 cloth; ISBN: 0-939416-39-5 9.95 paper.

The Shape of Red: Insider/Outsider Reflections by Ruth Hubbard and Margaret Randall. ISBN: 0-939416-19-0 24.95 cloth; ISBN: 0-939416-18-2 9.95 paper.

Women & Honor: Some Notes on Lying by Adrienne Rich. ISBN: 0-939416-44-1 3.95 paper.

ANIMAL RIGHTS

And a Deer's Ear, Eagle's Song and Bear's Grace: Relationships Between Animals and Women edited by Theresa Corrigan and Stephanie T. Hoppe. ISBN: 0-939416-38-7 24.95 cloth; ISBN: 0-939416-39-5 9.95 paper.

With a Fly's Eye, Whale's Wit and Woman's Heart: Relationships Between Animals and Women edited by Theresa Corrigan and Stephanie T. Hoppe. ISBN: 0-939416-24-7 24.95 cloth; ISBN: 0-939416-25-5 9.95 paper.

POLITICS OF HEALTH

The Absence of the Dead Is Their Way of Appearing by Mary Winfrey Trautmann. ISBN: 0-939416-04-2 8.95 paper.

AIDS: The Women edited by Ines Rieder and Patricia Ruppelt. ISBN: 0-939416-20-4 24.95 cloth; ISBN: 0-939416-21-2 9.95 paper

Don't: A Woman's Word by Elly Danica. ISBN: 0-939416-23-9 21.95 cloth; ISBN: 0-939416-22-0 8.95 paper

1 in 3: Women with Cancer Confront an Epidemic edited by Judith Brady. ISBN: 0-939416-50-6 24.95 cloth; ISBN: 0-939416-49-2 10.95 paper.

Voices in the Night: Women Speaking About Incest edited by Toni A. H. McNaron and Yarrow Morgan. ISBN: 0-939416-02-6 9.95 paper.

With the Power of Each Breath: A Disabled Women's Anthology edited by Susan Browne, Debra Connors and Nanci Stern.
ISBN: 0-939416-09-3 24.95 cloth;
ISBN: 0-939416-06-9 10.95 paper.

Woman-Centered Pregnancy and Birth by the Federation of Feminist Women's Health Centers.
ISBN: 0-939416-03-4 11.95 paper.

LESBIAN STUDIES

Boomer: Railroad Memoirs by Linda Niemann.
ISBN: 0-939416-55-7 12.95 paper.

Different Daughters: A Book by Mothers of Lesbians edited by Louise Rafkin.
ISBN: 0-939416-12-3 21.95 cloth;
ISBN: 0-939416-13-1 9.95 paper.

Different Mothers: Sons & Daughters of Lesbians Talk About Their Lives edited by Louise Rafkin.
ISBN: 0-939416-40-9 24.95 cloth;
ISBN: 0-939416-41-7 9.95 paper.

A Lesbian Love Advisor by Celeste West.
ISBN: 0-939416-27-1 24.95 cloth;
ISBN: 0-939416-26-3 9.95 paper.

Long Way Home: The Odyssey of a Lesbian Mother and Her Children by Jeanne Jullion.
ISBN: 0-939416-05-0 8.95 paper.

More Serious Pleasure: Lesbian Erotic Stories and Poetry edited by the Sheba Collective.
ISBN: 0-939416-48-4 24.95 cloth;
ISBN: 0-939416-47-6 9.95 paper.

The Night Audrey's Vibrator Spoke: A Stonewall Riots Collection by Andrea Natalie.
ISBN: 0-939416-64-6 8.95 paper.

Queer and Pleasant Danger: Writing Out My Life by Louise Rafkin.
ISBN: 0-939416-60-3 24.95 cloth;
ISBN: 0-939416-61-1 9.95 paper.

Serious Pleasure: Lesbian Erotic Stories and Poetry edited by the Sheba Collective.
ISBN: 0-939416-46-8 24.95 cloth;
ISBN: 0-939416-45-X 9.95 paper.

SEXUAL POLITICS

Good Sex: Real Stories from Real People by Julia Hutton.
ISBN: 0-939416-56-5 24.95 cloth;
ISBN: 0-939416-57-3 12.95 paper.

*Madonnarama: Essays on Sex
and Popular Culture* edited by
Lisa Frank and Paul Smith.
ISBN: 0-939416-72-7 24.95 cloth;
ISBN: 0-939416-71-9 9.95 paper.

*Sex Work: Writings by Women in
the Sex Industry*
edited by Frédérique Delacoste
and Priscilla Alexander.
ISBN: 0-939416-10-7 24.95 cloth;
ISBN: 0-939416-11-5 16.95 paper.

*Susie Bright's Sexual Reality: A
Virtual Sex World Reader*
by Susie Bright.
ISBN: 0-939416-58-1 24.95 cloth;
ISBN: 0-939416-59-X 9.95 paper.

Susie Sexpert's Lesbian Sex World
by Susie Bright.
ISBN: 0-939416-34-4 24.95 cloth;
ISBN: 0-939416-35-2 9.95 paper.

Since 1980, Cleis Press has published progressive books by
women. We welcome your order
and will ship your books as
quickly as possible. Individual
orders must be prepaid (U.S.
dollars only). Please add 15%
shipping. Pennsylvania residents
add 6% sales tax.

Mail orders: Cleis Press, P.O.
Box 8933, Pittsburgh PA 15221.
MasterCard and Visa orders:
include account number, exp.
date, and signature. Fax your
credit card order: (412) 937-1567.
Or, phone us Monday–Friday,
9 am–5 pm Eastern Standard
Time at (412) 937-1555.